PRAISE F

"Jeremy Robinson goes pedal to the metal into very dark territory!"
-- **Jonathan Maberry**

"Jeremy Robinson is the next James Rollins"
-- **Chris Kuzneski**

"If you like thrillers original, unpredictable and chock-full of action, you are going to love Jeremy Robinson..."
-- **Stephen Coonts**

"How do you find an original story idea in the crowded action-thriller genre? Two words: Jeremy Robinson."
-- **Scott Sigler**

"There's nothing timid about Robinson as he drops his readers off the cliff without a parachute and somehow manages to catch us an inch or two from doom."
-- **Jeff Long**

"Jeremy Robinson is an original and exciting voice."
-- **Steve Berry**

"Jeremy Robinson is a fresh new face in adventure writing and will make a mark in suspense for years to come."
--**David Lynn Golemon**

INSOMNIA

JEREMY ROBINSON

AUTHOR OF *INSTINCT* AND *PULSE*

BREAKNECK MEDIA

Visit Jeremy Robinson on the World Wide Web at:
www.jeremyrobinsononline.com

NOVELS by JEREMY ROBINSON

Threshold

The Last Hunter – Pursuit

The Last Hunter - Descent

Instinct

Pulse

Kronos

Antarktos Rising

Beneath

Raising the Past

The Didymus Contingency

INSOMNIA

INTRODUCTION

I don't write many short stories. In fact, the seven stories (plus one bonus) in INSOMNIA represent my entire collection of short stories. Before you call me lazy, keep in mind that I've written thirteen screenplays and just as many screenplay treatments, I have eight novels in print, four more in e-book (as of this writing—several more are on the way) and I write three to four books per year. So I don't have a lot of time for writing or selling shorts.

What this means is that all but three of these stories are exclusive to this collection. FROM ABOVE and HARDEN'S TREE were previously published in magazines, and BOUGHT AND PAID FOR is part of a podcast novel by Scott Sigler (see the story for details), but the rest have never been seen before.

There is no running theme between the stories, other than perhaps characters running for their lives. Most of the stories are experimental—I use first person perspective for many of them, which I typically don't do in my novels. And I touch on a variety of genres including action, horror, science fiction, sci-fi noir and even romantic thriller. The result is an interesting mishmash of stories that match my novels in intensity, action and thrills, but touch on subjects and themes I might normally shy away from.

For those that are interested, I've provided brief afterwords at the end of each story, detailing what I remember about its writing and what I think about the story now.

I hope you enjoy all seven stories and the bonus story. Thanks for reading!

-- Jeremy Robinson

INSOMNIA

"What's good about it?" I say, in response to George's peppy *Good Morning*.

"You wake up on the wrong side of bed?" George asks.

I shoot George an angry glance.

"Just a joke," George says. "You forget your Feene today?"

George is a kind man, but he's always butting into other peoples' business. The shift just started and he's already running off at the mouth.

"You're kidding, right? I haven't got into any trouble since I was a kid."

George leans in close, like we're pals, and says, "I heard Jep, down in shipping, missed his Feene jump at the beginning of the shift. People say he's looking pale...sick-like."

My hands freeze above the production line and three ducks get past me without heads attached. "Damnit."

"Don't worry about them, Henderson," George says, "Missing a few duck heads isn't like not taking your Feene. Think Jep will make the twelve hours before the next jump?"

George is really getting on my nerves. *I missed three in a row!* Of course, technically I had only missed two, because I usually go every other one. When I'm first in line I like to give the other fellas a break. There are four of them after me. They'd probably like having a few more heads to put on, but I enjoy picking up the slack for other people—just the kind of guy I am.

I look to my right and see a line of fifty men, some attaching duck heads, some attaching wings, some painting beaks orange, all so every kid in the world can have the same new duck.

I remember my duck. Seems to me the orange on the beaks was brighter back then. Everything was brighter back then. George keeps talking, maybe fifteen minutes before he realizes I'm not listening anymore. Damn managers are all the same. All talk and no work. Sometimes I wonder why they even need the Feene...they got all the time in the world to sleep.

Sleep.

I push the word out of my head and go back to work.

Pick up the duck.

Put on the head.

Put the duck down.

Pick up the duck.

Put on the head.

Put the duck down.

Nine hours of the same.

I know my ten hours are almost up when my arms start to shake and my eyes begin to blur. Nothing a little Feene can't fix, but it will be two more hours before we get another jump. Just enough time to walk home, eat, shave, shower and walk back. Then the next shift begins and we do the same thing again, seven days a week, every day of the year. It's a living.

The bell rings right on time. I finish the duck in my hand, put it on the conveyor belt and turn toward the door. The fifty other men working the belt with me shuffle toward the door at the same time, falling into a natural formation that has sort of just happened over the past twenty years.

Once we reach the courtyard, we're hit by a burst of cool air that occasionally wafts in from the ocean. I pause at the door and take a deep breath. The air is sweet. Someone bumps me from behind. "C'mon Henderson, you're putting us a few seconds back."

I enter the courtyard and take my usual place in the growing crowd of hundreds of men, all filing out of various doors around the Happy Duck fabrication building. I'm almost to the gate when I see him.

Jep.

He looks like hell, stumbling forward, bumping into men. His swollen eyes are surrounded by dark rings. I've never seen a man who's missed a Feene jump, but I know the second I see him—Jep's in trouble. He's five single file lines away. Too far for me reach him before passing through the gates.

It's another three minutes before I hit the sidewalk and turn to walk down my street. I glance back, thinking of Jep, and I catch a glimpse of him spilling out of the factory gate. His feet look heavy and his head is rolling around like a newborn baby's. I see his eyes close, and a panic sweeps across my body.

Jep lurches forward and begins to fall, but I'm still quick enough to catch the man. After dogging past three workers and bounding the rest of the distance in four steps, I clutch him in my arms and push him back to his feet. I've never woken anyone up before, and I'm not sure what to do. I slap him hard across the face.

"Jep! Snap out of it!"

Jep's eyes launch open for a moment and then sink back down, but he's awake. He must have realized that he'd slept, because he gets jittery, real quick. "Oh God. I wasn't asleep, was I?"

The look in my eyes tells him that he was.

"No...I was only a few minutes late...I was sick!"

"Sick? The Feene takes care of that."

"It was something I ate...." Jep looks at the ground. "I...I had to take a second shower."

"Forget about it," I say. "You weren't in REM sleep, so you're okay."

"You sure?"

"Yes." I lie. I've never seen someone in REM sleep before. "You don't hear any sirens do you?"

We listen and hear nothing but the hundreds of feet walking away from Happy Duck. He relaxes.

"C'mon," I say. "Come to my place, and I'll keep you awake until the next jump."

"I don't think I can go two more hours."

I smile, "I have something that will keep you awake."

It takes us fifteen minutes to walk to my house; five minutes longer than usual. And it was five minutes before we headed out... I assume it will take just as long to get back, because he'll be even more tired. That leaves me with an hour and twenty minutes...a full twenty minutes less than I'm used to.

I practically drag Jep into the house and sit him down at the kitchen table. He looks ready to pass out again, but he perks up some when he gets a whiff of what I'm brewing. He sits up straight.

"What's that smell?"

I pour a cup and bring it to him. He smells the dark liquid and looks momentarily revitalized. "It...it smells incredible!"

He's already waking up.

Jep takes a sip of the steamy liquid, then another and another, with each gulp looking more aware of his surroundings. He observes the contents of my kitchen, taking in the stainless steel fridge, dishwasher and sink, but after taking another sip, his attention is brought back to the drink. "You have to tell me, Henderson, what is this?"

I smile. "Coffee."

As expected, Jep spits out the coffee in his mouth and wipes his face with his sleeve. "Coffee is illegal!"

I nod.

"But you can...how did you get it? Why do you...?" Jep looks back at the coffee and smiles. "Where can I get some?" He takes a long drag and sets the mug back on the table. "So this is what they used in the old days, huh? I have to say, it feels better than what they give us now."

"Lacks the punch," I say. "This will tide you over until the next jump, but you'll be worse off than when you began once it wears off. I keep it in the house for when I'm feeling a bit slow."

He smiles and says, "Your secret's safe with me. I won't tell a soul."

"Thanks."

"I mean it," Jep says. "I owe you for this."

"You can repay me by taking a shower double time so I can get one in before the next shift starts."

George chugs his remaining coffee, and I point him toward the bathroom.

When I hear the water turn on I head to the changing room, what I remember my parents calling a bedroom, only adults weren't allowed to have beds...also against the law. Beds encourage sleep. Sleep leads to dreams. Dreams lead to chaos.

Our society has become a crime-free utopia thanks to Feene. No one has dreams. Everyone works. We have become an all-efficient world that can pump out a million ducks a week. And beds aren't part of the picture...for anyone—

But me.

I open the door to my bedroom and plop down on my bed.

It's soft.

It's warm.

It's *Heaven*.

It took me five years to build, rushing to the lumber yard to pick up scraps during my two-hour breaks and assembling a frame from what I remembered of my childhood. Kids could sleep...until they were eight. Then they go on Feene like the rest of us, go to school in ten-hour shifts like the rest of us and eventually go to work like the rest of us.

It is perfect.

We all have houses.

We all have food.

We all have work.

There was a time when some people had none of the above. Not anymore.

I close my eyes and pretend to sleep, knowing full well that it's impossible with the Feene still in my system. I roll over onto my stomach, feeling the soft cushion I'd fashioned from years of old clothes, sewn and taped together. It's ugly as hades, but for me, it's the softest thing my body has ever touched.

Laying here with my eyes closed, I let my mind drift. A smile creeps onto my face as I remember my youth...my yellow duck. But then my mind drifts further...to the smell. The sweet smell I had experienced after leaving Happy Duck earlier today. Where had it come from? I let my mind follow the possibilities, and I begin seeing a land covered in grass, with trees and animals. The wind blows through the trees and pulls the fragrance toward my nose. I can smell it again. A tear forms in my eye.

They can keep me from sleeping, but they can't keep me from dreaming.

I shoot to my feet and listen, holding my breath. The water is off.

After wiping my eye dry, I sneak out the door.

Jep stands in the kitchen, toweling his hair dry. I look at the clock. A half hour has passed. Not enough time left for me to take a shower.

"Sorry I took so long," he says, rubbing his eyes. "I'm still moving a little slow."

"Don't worry about it. Won't be the first time I skipped a shower for a little snooze."

Jep's eyes open wide. "What?"

I laugh out loud. "Joking."

Jeps laughs nervously.

I fix some food and we eat it as quickly as possible before heading out. We have twenty minutes before my shift starts, twenty three before Jep's.

The walk ends up taking twenty-one minutes.

We're in line at the jump station, which looks like toll booth resized for people. I show my card as usual and wait for the jump. Nothing happens. I turn to the attendant, forehead wrinkled. "Sorry," he says. "You're late, and efficiency rules are efficiency rules. You'll have to do without for this shift."

I just stare at him. I've never missed a jump before.

The attendant reaches past me and scans Jep's card. A second later he produces a gel-cap pill, filled with a rainbow swirl of liquid. I begin to salivate as I watch Jep eagerly swallow the pill down. Jep looks at me apologetically. "Sorry about that. I'll help you home

when the shift is out."

I head for my section and turn back to Jep. "Don't worry about me," I say in an almost whisper. "I had enough coffee to keep me wide awake for two shifts." I hold my index finger to my lips and shush loudly with a smile.

Jep smiles, but mine fades away as I approach the conveyor.

Pick up the duck.

Put on the head.

Put the duck down.

Sleep.

Pick up the duck.

Put on the head.

Put the duck down.

Sleep.

My eyes grow heavy, but I continue on, concentrating on the task at hand; *put the duck head on for ten hours without Feene, without sleeping, and you'll be fine*, I tell myself.

My hands become shaky, and hope seeps into my mind. My hands never get shaky until the shift is up. I glance at the clock. Only three hours have passed.

The next time I look at the clock, only a half hour more has passed, then fifteen minutes, then five. Time is slowing down. And I'm missing ducks. I look to my right and see the four other guys working the duck heads moving fast, picking up the ducks I missed, which is most of them.

"You okay, Henderson?" someone asks, but I can't tell who.

"Missed his Feene," someone else says.

I focus on the ducks, willing my hands to move faster.

Pick up the duck.

Put on the head.

Put the duck down.

Pick up the duck.

Put on the head.

Put the duck down.

My fingers slip, and I drop the duck to the floor. I bend over to pick it up. I feel a wave of nausea pass through my body from head to toe. It's like nothing I've ever felt before.

Sleep.

I jolt back up and come face to face with George, smiling wide. "Missed your Feene, Henderson? Everyone's talking about it. I heard you helped Jep make it through the break. Looks like it's your turn, eh?"

George continues to talk, but I don't hear him. I close my eyes for an instant and open them again. A voice inside my head shouts at me to close them again, to sleep. I attach another duck head, but I never put it back down.

I blink.

When my eyes open again, I'm looking at the ceiling. Then George, who is leaning over me, shouts something unintelligible. I realize then that I had fallen asleep—really fallen asleep! I urge my arms and legs to push me up, to stand, but nothing happens.

I blink again.

I think I hear something, shouting maybe, and then a pressure squeezes under both my arms. It's...comfortable.

A loud noise makes me open my eyes, and I realize I'm no longer in the factory. I'm lying on my back, on a cement slab. Two feet...two black, shiny shoes are in front of my face. I look up to see a grim man with a dark mustache peering down at me.

"Where am I?"

"Where you ought to be."

"I'm in jail?"

"Penal colony."

"No..."

"Should have thought of that before you went to sleep."

"It was an accident."

The man looks down at me, his lips turned down. "We found your bed."

I stare at the floor, unable to face the man again.

"This is where you belong. All you sleepers are alike."

"Please, I—"

"You want to sleep? You want to dream?"

"Dreams...are good."

The man laughs. "You belong here. You want chaos? You got it. For you, Feene is a thing of the past."

The door slams behind the man as he leaves. I feel an incredible sadness, but I refuse to keep my eyes open any longer.

I awake feeling better, almost like I'd just had a jump. But I know I haven't. The pale cement walls remind me where I am—what I did. Light streams into the box of a room from a window above my head. It seems unusually bright...and it's getting brighter.

The sun is rising. I slept through the night.

I'm suddenly struck, though not from a fist or anything else quite so physical. It's a smell.

The smell.

I suck a deep breath into my lungs, allowing the sweet smell to tickle my nose. The fragrance floats thick in the air.

Creak.

The door opens.

"Hello?"

No one responds.

Creak.

The door opens some more and then sways back and forth. A cool breeze hits me, carrying more of the wonderful odor. The door is open. *What kind of prison cell is this?*

I walk to the door and peer out into the brightness beyond.

I must still be sleeping.

This is my dream...my awake dream...it's come into my sleeping dreams.

I step out onto the ground, which sinks beneath my feet. I look down. *Sand?* I'd seen sand a few times as a child, but I never touched it, never experienced it. I bend down and take a handful of the sand, letting it run through my fingers. It's cold and soft.

I glance to my right and see fifty square cells, just like my own, spaced out along the beach. But the others are decorated with leaves, potted plants...flowers! The smell must be flowers! My heart pounds in my chest, surging blood through my veins faster than any Feene-jump I've ever had.

Then I see the people. Some lounge in hammocks. Some are

fishing. And some splash around in the water...in the ocean. And they're laughing. Really laughing. I walk to the side of my cell and gaze out at the ocean. The water's so blue it stings my eyes. The sky dances with glowing clouds. I can hear the trees rustling in the wind and a cool air massages my skin. And still the smell lingers.

Then, waddling by the shore is a duck. A real duck. Its green head shines like an emerald and its little knobby orange legs kick out one at a time, carrying it forward. Its feathers are an assortment of browns, grays and whites. It lets out a little quack and waddles into the water.

I fall to my knees, in awe. I rub my eyes to make sure my vision is clear.

When I open my eyes again I see a pair of bare feet standing in front of me. I look up to see a beautiful woman with flowing white hair. She's wearing what appears to be a hand-made bikini top and a pair of short, tattered shorts that does little to hide her bronzed legs. She smiles at me with gleaming teeth. "See where dreams get you?" she says.

I laugh the truest laugh of my life and begin to weep as the bright sunflower-sun rises over my new world, where ducks aren't all yellow.

AFTERWORD

Sometimes authors use fiction to sort through, emote and otherwise deal with issues in their own lives. Insomnia is one such issue. I have gone three days with only three hours of sleep between them. I routinely lay in bed at night for hours, before falling asleep—often until after the sun has risen. My average amount of sleep per night is five hours.

The result is a craving for something that is forbidden to me, not by the constraints of a workaholic future society, but by my own frenetic mind and overactive imagination, which dreams up many of the horrible scenarios I write about while I should be sleeping. In addition to that, I have a sensory processing disorder (which I gave to the character, Sara Fogg, in my novel, INSTINCT).

So what does this disorder do that keeps me awake? Primarily, I FEEL sounds. It is especially troublesome at night when there is very little background noise. The ping and pop of heat coming on feels like a punch in the stomach. A baby's cry (I have three) twists my gut. Absolutely everything I hear at night opens my eyes and sets my heart racing.

Another effect of SPD is that my imagination, which is hard to reign in while laying in the dark, can actually create a spike in adrenaline, which makes it impossible to sleep, sometimes even while on something as potent as Ambien!

Henderson's plight, of craving sleep, of longing to close his eyes and dream, matches my own. I would love to be able to simply lie down, close my eyes and sleep. If only my Feene pill wasn't hard wired into my mind!

On the plus side, most of the stories in the collection were written late at night while the rest of my household slept. So maybe something good has come of it.

THE EATER

On a particularly hot summer day in New Hampshire, a small pool of water sat alone in a sandy, tree-surrounded clearing. Torrential rains had flooded a nearby stream, which overflowed into a neighboring bog. The flooding expanded, pushing water and transplanting fish, amphibians and various other swamp dwellers into the normally parched clearing. For the first few days, the area became a temporary oasis, but the sun had been burning bright for five days now and all that remained of the flood was a single, one-foot deep, inky black pool that churned continuously like a boiling brew.

Surrounded by tall pine trees, the clearing remained unknown to many, save for a few junk dumpers and an adventurous child or two. In this case—three.

Matthew, the oldest of the three brothers wore thick glasses that acted like a magnifying glass when held just right in the sun's beams. The siblings had learned the trick last summer and it brought them to the clearing again this summer. The clearing was chock full of ants fit for roasting. Joshua, the youngest, was still only six years old, but he had the lungs of an opera singer, shouting about anything that crossed his path. The middle of the trio, Jerry, was, for today at least, the ring leader.

"This sucks," Matthew said as he swung a pine branch around his head, shooing away the mosquitoes. "I can't even see the ants squirming."

"You can see them when they're dead," Jerry said as he led his brothers through the last of the pine trees and into the clearing.

"That's dumb. If I want to see dead ants I can just squish them with my finger when I'm wearing my glasses."

"C'mon," Jerry said, "humor your dying brother."

Matthew gave Jerry an angry look. "That's not funny. You're not going to die."

Jerry kicked the dirt. "Kids with leukemia die, Matt."

Matthew opened his mouth to continue the argument, but he was cut short. "Guys! Guys!" It was Joshua. "Look at this pine cone. It's huge!"

Matthew and Jerry cringed as Joshua's high voice tore across the forest like a lighthouse cuts through fog.

"Shut up!" Matthew said as he pushed past the last of the pine branches and stepped into the clearing. "If you don't shut up, we're not bringing you with us next time."

"But this pine cone is huge!" Joshua said. With his eyes glued to the pine cone in his hands, Joshua failed to notice his brothers had frozen at the outer perimeter of the clearing. "Oh! Eww...There's yellow stuff on it! Really, you guys should—oof!" Joshua tripped over Jerry's sneakered foot and crashed to the ground, sending a cloud of dusty soil into the air.

Joshua sat up and brushed himself off. "I'm telling Mom! You two..." Joshua looked up at Matthew and Jerry, who normally would have teased him about his unfortunate fall by now, and saw that they hadn't even noticed him on the ground. That wouldn't do. "Hey! Hello! I'm telling Mom you pushed me!"

Nothing.

Joshua's forehead furrowed in confusion. It was then that Jerry turned to Matthew. "Should we get Dad?"

"Dad's not going to help you when I tell mom you pushed me," Joshua said, looking up from his place on the ground.

Jerry looked down at Joshua. His eyes were wide. "Josh...what?"

"I'm telling Mom you pushed me..." Joshua said.

Jerry just looked confused.

Joshua's forehead grew wrinkled. "What?"

"Josh...look." Jerry said, returning his gaze to the clearing.

Joshua turned and looked out at the clearing. He leapt to his feet and let out a shrill scream. "Oh! That's gross, that's gross, that's gross!"

"Shut up!" Matthew said, taking a step forward. "I think we should get out of here."

Jerry strode past Matthew, bent down and inspected one of the hundreds of miniature corpses littering the clearing. "It's a salamander," Jerry said.

Matthew and Joshua seemed to be put at ease that the dead creatures could be identified. They moved forward.

"Gross and gross," Josh said as he looked at a dead frog.

Matthew bent down to a large rainbow trout and poked it with
the end of his pine branch. "Man, I could've caught this guy."

"No way," Josh said. "I would have caught him first."

Matthew snickered. "You couldn't catch your tail if you had one.
Idiot."

"I'm telling Mom!"

"Shut up!"

"Guys, look," Jerry said as he walked deeper into the clearing,
hopping past small, crispy corpses as he moved. "There's some water."

"I don't think that's a good idea," Matthew said.

Jerry quickened his pace. "Chicken?"

"Yeah!" Josh said, heading into the corpse field. "You're a chick-
en!"

Matthew sighed and followed his brothers toward the center of
the clearing, where he could see a pool of water.

Jerry was leaning over the water when Matthew and Joshua arrived. "What do you think they are?" Jerry said.

Joshua stuck his tongue out. "They're gross."

"If you say the word 'gross' one more time, I'm gonna throw you
in there," Matthew said.

Joshua pursed his lips.

Matthew looked at the water. It was full of squirming, slippery,
wet creatures that made the water as dark as oil. "Tadpoles? We

found tadpoles in a puddle a few years ago."

"I don't think they're tadpoles," Jerry said.

"Okay, genius, what are they?"

Jerry leaned closer. "I don't know...I'll catch one."

"I don't think you should," Matthew said. "What if they're poisonous?"

Jerry poised his hand over the water. "There's nothing poisonous in New Hampshire."

"Rattlesnakes," Joshua said. "Dad says there were rattlesnakes on Rattlesnake Mountain, until all the people went up there and killed them."

"They're not snakes," Jerry said, shaking his head.

Matthew chuckled. "Idiot...And don't say you're telling!"

Joshua huffed and crossed his arms.

Jerry lowered his arm over the pool, took a deep breath and then plunged his hand into the water. Moving quickly, he attempted several times to grab hold of something. "I can't catch them! They're squirming out of my hand."

Joshua crinkled his nose and stepped back. Matthew gritted his teeth as he watched and adjusted his glasses to make sure he saw everything clearly.

"Got one!" Jerry said. He pulled his arm up and then suddenly stopped. The black water wriggled up over Jerry's hand and wrapped around his wrist. He tried to pull his arm out of the pool, but the water's grip was strong.

Jerry looked back at Matthew with wide eyes.

"Help." It was only a whisper.

Before Matthew could take action, Jerry was yanked into the pool. He splashed down into the water, kicking his legs and flailing his arms, screaming the entire time.

Matthew turned to Joshua, who was also screaming at the top of his lungs. "Get Dad!"

Matthew shouted, on the verge of panic. "Get Dad, now!"

Joshua turned and ran as fast as he could, yelling, "Dad! Dad!"

Matthew turned back to the pool and found Jerry was no longer thrashing. On his back, Jerry lay partially submerged, staring at the sky.

"Jerry?"

Nothing.

Matthew bent down to him. His skin grew bluer by the second and then his eyes glanced at Matt's and he moved his mouth. "Wa...ter."

Matthew grabbed Jerry's shirt and pulled him from the pool. "Wa...ter!" Jerry said.

Looking at the water, Matthew sensed that something had gone terribly wrong. He gazed at Jerry's blue skin, wondering if the leukemia somehow attacked his brother's body. But then he noticed something else. Jerry's abdomen had swelled, and it moved, churning, just like the water back at the clearing did. Matthew looked back at the pool.

The water was crystal clear.

Matthew's face contorted into absolute fear as he looked back at Jerry, realizing that whatever lived in the pool, now squirmed inside his brother's body, choking the life out of him, maybe even eating him alive.

"Water," Jerry said again. "Hurry."

Matthew sucked in a quick breath as the message became clear in his mind. He reached down, picked Jerry up by his armpits and began dragging him toward the woods. "The stream is just through the woods," he said. "We'll make it."

But Jerry slumped down, limp in Matthew's hands.

For five minutes, Matthew grunted and groaned as he dragged Jerry through the woods. Jerry's skin was cold and turning purple. Matthew's eyes watered as he feared the worst. His brother was dead.

Without warning, the soil beneath Matthew's feet gave way and he fell backward, letting go of Jerry as he careened downward. He struck water a moment later—the stream. Coughing and spitting, Matthew came to the surface gasping for air and missing his glasses. He looked up and saw the blurry figure of Jerry hanging over the edge of the embankment.

Though positive it was too late, Matthew knew he had to try. He reached up and took Jerry by the hand. Gravity was on Matthew's side now, and he pulled Jerry into the water with one fast tug. Jerry splashed into the water and lay face up above the surface. He wasn't moving.

Matthew punched the water with his fists. "Jerry! Wake up!"

Then Jerry moved, but only a subtle movement. He opened his mouth. Matthew barely saw it through his blurred vision.

Matthew's terror rose as a terrible thought entered his mind. To save his brother, he'd have to drown him.

Tears flowing freely from Matthew's face, he took Jerry by the shoulders and thrust him beneath the water. Jerry began kicking and thrashing just as he had in the pool of water. Through clouded vision, Matthew witnessed the water around them turn black. The dark water spread out wide and then dissipated. Jerry's body stopped writhing.

A hand launched out of the water and gripped Matthew's arm. He shouted and pulled Jerry from the water. Coughing wildly, Jerry clambered to the muddy embankment and continued to hack and wheeze for a full minute.

When it was over, he turned to Matthew, who had just recovered his glasses from the stream bed. "Thanks."

"Are you okay?"

Jerry nodded. "They were leeches, I think."

"Leeches?"

Jerry nodded again. "We better get out of the water."

The pair scrambled up the embankment and managed to hobble out to one of the only paved roads for miles. They began to hike back toward the cabin their family stayed in every summer when a loud horn made them jump.

A green station wagon screeched to a stop next to them. Matthew and Jerry sighed with relief. Their father climbed out of the driver's-side door and headed toward them. Joshua poked his head out of the backseat window. "I got Mom and Dad!"

"At least you're good for something," Matthew said.

Jerry passed out and collapsed into his father's arms, exhausted from the ordeal. "What happened?" their father demanded.

"He's okay," Matthew said.

The father grimaced. "Get in the car."

Matthew got in the backseat with Joshua, knowing that they would all be in trouble for this later on. "Where are we going?" he asked as their father placed Jerry next to their mother on the front seat. "The hospital," their mother said.

The doors closed and the car zoomed through the woods, arriving at the nearest hospital twenty minutes later. Jerry remained unconscious when the doctors began testing him; they closed the doors to the examination room and asked the family to wait outside as they preformed more tests.

For three hours, their parents, Matthew and Joshua lingered in the waiting room, pacing, chewing their lips and wringing their hands together, but no one spoke. The door to the room opened and a doctor approached. Matthew noticed the odd expression on the doctor's face. Something was wrong.

"I'm afraid I don't quite understand what happened here today," the doctor said.

All eyes remained glued to the doctor's. He continued, "Your son, Jerry...We got his medical history from the Children's Hospital in Boston."

The mother nodded. "That's where he's being treated."

"Then the charts are correct? Jerry had leukemia?"

The father nodded. "Jerry *has* leukemia."

The doctor flashed a toothy grin. "*Had* leukemia. Whatever happened to him out there today...his blood is clean...the cancer is gone."

Matthew's jaw dropped open and he bolted for Jerry's room. The parents careened after him. Joshua stood alone in the hallway with the doctor. He looked up at the doctor and removed an object from his pocket. He held it up for the doctor to see. "Want to see my pine cone? It's huge!"

AFTERWORD

Rereading this story after so long brought a smile to my face. Everything in it, except for the leukemia and leeches is a part of me. Matthew is my older brother. Joshua is my younger brother. And Jerry is me. The dynamic between the three brothers and the way they speak to each other is all very accurate. Even the green station wagon is an icon of my youth.

We spent all of our childhood summers at a campground in New Hampshire (which I also featured prominently in my novel PULSE). The stream is there, and Matthew really did fall into it one summer. He was trapped and I had to run back to the cabin for help. Ironically, the person who came to our aid was...Aunt Jerry. No joke. The flooded sandpit is real and begins most summers full of water. By midsummer it is reduced to a large puddle that absolutely swarms with writhing tadpoles. That puddle was the inspiration for this story.

I wrote this story after moving back to New Hampshire from Los Angles. Wanting to reconnect with nature after having lived in the city for three years, my wife and I spent the summer at the cabin. I was surrounded by the sights, sounds and smells of my childhood and turned them into this story. Reading it brings back a lot of good memories of places and experiences that still inspire my writing today.

HARDEN'S TREE

"He was pure evil," Jamie said, as she stared up at the leafless maple.

Standing beside her, I noticed how the roots cling to the ground on top of the grassy hill, like a massive hand squeezing the guts out of the Earth. "I don't believe a word of it," I said. "And I'm not getting any closer."

Jamie was eighteen; two years older than me and a dream come true. When she asked me to go for a walk tonight, I nearly passed out. Then I found out Chaz was coming—her boyfriend, who stood waiting at the top of the one hundred foot-tall hill. *Damn.*

Jamie smiled at me, "C'mon, Ben. You're not afraid of an old tree, are you?"

"No," I said. That was the first lie I ever told her.

Jamie shook her head and joined Chaz at the base of the tree, next to the bronze plaque. I'd never read it personally, but I knew what it said. "Here lie the ashes of Harden Holt – Who in the year of our Lord, 1897, did murder twenty-six Christians with a sharpened stick."

Everyone told the story around here, and not just on Halloween—all the time. It was Rumsfield, New Hampshire's claim to fame. Harden murdered those people, it was true. The townspeople hung him and after he was dead, they burned his body, buried the ashes on top of this hill and planted a tree over the sight. It was supposed to be symbolic—something about representing new life from death.

But the only thing kept alive by the planting of this tree was the story of Harden himself. Every year that maple tree grew taller and spread its branches wide, but never once did it sprout leaves. Most people say it's on account of Harden's ashes being buried there. Some people say the tree is alive...possessed by his spirit. Whatever the case, I don't like it.

I looked back down the hill, toward the road and thought about heading back home. Chaz was probably gonna drool all over Jamie anyways and I didn't feel like watching.

"Wimp!" It was Chaz. "I didn't think you had the gonads to come up here!"

I could hear him laughing and I spun around to spew insults, but instead I saw something odd behind the tree. The sky was growing dark with spongy clouds.

"What're you looking at?" Jamie asked.

I pointed beyond Jamie, toward the sky. "Storm's coming."

Chaz and Jamie looked at the sky. "Aww, that's nothing," Chaz said. "Listen, why don't you go home and hide in the basement. Jamie and I have a lot to talk about, don't we, babe?" With that, Chaz swatted her butt, drawing a giggle from Jamie's mouth.

I frowned. Maybe Jamie wasn't the girl for me. Any woman who can be aroused by a rump slapping from a jerk who enjoys taunting younger and smaller guys wasn't worth my time.

As I turned and walked down the hill, listening to the pitiful lovebirds' chortle, the rain began to fall. It fell slowly at first, but then it turned into a reenactment of Noah's flood.

Stepping on the pavement made me feel safe. I turned back and wiped the wet hair from my forehead. Jamie and Chaz were coming back down the hill, holding their hands over their faces like it would stop the wetness from sinking into their pores.

Then, the hair on my arms rose up as a blast of wind surged over the top of the hill, bending the limbs of the tree so that each looked like a fishing pole holding a thirty-pound largemouth. *Snap!* I saw one of the branches break free and launch down the hill like a javelin.

A second later, the branch protruded from Chaz's chest. He fell onto the wet grass and slid five feet, leaving a slick trail of plasma behind him. Chaz was dead.

Before I had time to scream or run, a bright flash filled the air and twin streaks of lightning appeared in the sky above the tree. Sparks flew and the trunk of the massive maple groaned. Harden's tree toppled toward me like a...well, like a falling tree. I jumped back even though I was well out of range.

But Jamie wasn't.

She let out a quick scream before the limbs of the crashing tree smashed her to the ground and impaled her in several places.

I ran as fast as I could and didn't stop until I reached the State Police barracks out on 93. I ran through the station doors and vomited, which garnered their undivided attention. After explaining the tragedy, I headed back out to Harden's Tree with two officers. When we arrived, the grass and road were still wet from the rainstorm, which had disappeared.

I gasped when I looked for Harden's tree. The grass on the hill was flattened, revealing that something had fallen here, but the tree was gone—the bodies too.

I hiked to the top of the hill with the officers and stopped five feet short of where the tree once stood. I expected to see the tree stump where it had been severed, but only a crater remained. Every root was missing, pulled clean from the ground like hair tugged out of skin.

While the officers took photos and talked about what could have happened, I noticed a glint of metal shining in the morning sun. I bent down, picked up the curiosity and dusted it off. It was the plaque. I read it for myself for the first time. "Here lie the ashes of Harden Holt – Who in the year of our Lord, 1897, did murder twenty-six Christians with a sharpened stick." But there was something else there, an arrow etched into the metal. I followed the arrow and flipped the plaque over. Scratched into the metal was a message, "Twenty-eight, if you're still counting."

AFTERWORD

When I sat down to write Harden's Tree, I had no idea about what I was going to write. I simply had a challenge—to write something interesting, entertaining, and perhaps a little frightening in one thousand words or less. I honestly can't recall why I felt the need to hit a one thousand word count. Perhaps it was a requirement of the magazine that eventually published the story. Perhaps it was because, for a long time, I didn't think good stories could be told in less than one thousand words (of course, maybe you'll agree with that now).

But I'm happy with the results and after having read the story again after six years, I find my imagination conjuring up where Harden's Tree got off to. Is it sitting in some forest, just waiting for unsuspecting hikers? Are the descendents of the people who hung Harden waking up to find a new, barren tree in their backyards? Is it hunting down anyone obnoxious enough to have the name Chaz?

If your name is Chaz, my apologies. But seriously, watch out for leafless trees.

STAR CROSSED KILLERS

I swim along the port side of the yacht undetected. My kicks are small but effective. My arms hang limp to my sides, one with a bullet hole, the other tingling awake after being wrapped in a buoy line for almost an hour.

I kick harder with the knowledge that my shoulder is oozing a trail of blood into the Pacific Ocean ten miles off the coast of Los Angeles. I half expect a great white to rise from the depths and swallow me whole. With the day I'm having, I wouldn't doubt it.

The job was simple. Kill the dealer; steal the statue. Simple, right?

Would have been if not for her.

Samantha.

She beat me to it. Hired by the competition. She's a Jack of all trades, like me—thief, spy, assassin—whatever the job calls for. And like me, she never fails.

For years we simply admired each others' work from a distance, looking for signs of the other's handiwork in the evening news. Chance brought us together a year ago. We were breaking into the same museum in search of different prizes. Without a word shared between us, we worked our way into the museum, got what we needed and then shared a bed. We didn't speak, not one word.

There was no need. We knew we'd see each other again.

And we did.

Ten times in the last year.

By the fifth encounter we were speaking. By the tenth, we were sharing our dreams for the future—and our fears.

Like the one being played out today.

We don't share information on jobs until after they're complete so neither of us expected to see the other today. But when our eyes met outside the auction house, we both knew the score. I didn't fail. She didn't fail. But today, one of us would. It was a code for us, like Bushido, and if one of us died in obedience to that code, so be it.

If you're not going to do something right, my father used to say.

Still, we're human. Her distraction over my presence allows me to retrieve the statue first. It's a solid gold number. Aztec or Mayan, I think. I don't really know and don't much care. What I do know is that it's priceless to my client.

But I was slow, my thoughts on Samantha's tarnished reputation. She catches up with me on the docks. Puts a bullet in my shoulder, takes the statue and kicks me into the ocean.

A mistake. She should have killed me. I know this. She will soon.

My kicking creates a tiny splash. I stop and listen. Not a sound. Sam and her two guards are below deck, confident that no one could get the jump on them with miles of ocean on every side. I'm not sure what they're doing out here, but I'm pretty sure it's to make the drop to her employer. That can never happen.

I roll up onto the rear dive platform and wait for most of the water to drip away from my body before risking a peek. When I do, I'm surprised to see one of the guards standing on the rear deck. The man must be deaf, I think, or just not accustomed to the sounds of ocean. The green tone of his skin and his look of disgust as he wanders over to the port rail and loses his lunch confirms it. Had I been a minute slower, he would have vomited on my head.

I leap up onto the rear deck. The sound of my feet on the hard-wood floor is masked by his heaving. He straightens and wipes his mouth with his arm, which makes a convenient gag. The whole attack takes three seconds. I pull his arm tight against his mouth and poke my four inch blade into both his lungs. Before his shock has worn off and the realization that he's going to die sets in, I tip him forward and lower him into the ocean. If the sharks don't get him, he'll surface in a few days. Maybe wash up in Santa Barbara.

I wipe my knife clean on a beach towel hanging over a lounge chair.

We made love in a chair like that once. Me and Sam.

Brazil.

Rio.

It was hot. And humid. More so than now.

As my mind traces the curves of her body, I find myself feeling something totally foreign to me—remorse. Not for the things I've done, but for what I'm about to do.

"What are you doing here, Sean?"

Or not.

She sounds surprised and angry. She had to know I wouldn't give up.

I turn to find her holding two black backpacks, and I realize my mistake. The drop had already taken place. Her employer was on this yacht. What I can't figure out is why she didn't just kill me. People think that shooting someone in the back lacks honor. I know better. It's an act of mercy. People who don't see death coming die at peace. Sometimes with a smile on their face. But those that do see it coming, who look the assassin in the eyes or stare down the barrel of a gun, they endure the worst torture imaginable—the knowledge that they are about to die.

I have no such worries, however. I can throw my knife faster than she can raise her gun.

Why hasn't she raised her gun?

We stare at each other, each waiting for the other to make a move. I risk a glance at her body. She's nearly six feet tall and a mixture of curves and straight lines in all the right places. She's changed her clothes. I catch a whiff of soap. Washed her hands, too.

Then she disarms me. Not with a shot. Not with a kick. Instead, she drops her weapon. She *drops* her weapon. Her fate is sealed. Or is it? Because I'm suddenly consumed with guilt. She is sacrificing herself, for me? This is *not* the code.

"What are you doing?" I ask, angry that she's not going to at least *try* to kill me.

"Saving you."

"I don't need—"

"I could have killed you."

I didn't argue. She was right.

"You should have."

"Are you going to kill me?" she asks, raising an eyebrow.

I don't answer. I don't need to.

"How many are below deck?" I ask.

"Two, but they're both dead."

I'm confused again. Why would she kill her employer? Why would she—? I finally see the truth of what's happening. She *is* saving me. And she's not doing it by sacrificing her life, she's sacrificing her reputation.

Now I'm pissed. "What's in the bags?"

She opens the first. Money. At least a million dollars. Instead of opening the second, she tosses it to me. "That one is yours," she says.

I don't need to open it. I can tell what it is by the weight.

It's one of the rare occasions in my life that I've felt loved. And for a moment, I enjoy it. Then we're dragging bodies across the deck and dumping them into the ocean. With the job complete, she takes the helm and throttles the yacht back to port.

We're silent on the way back.

We're almost always silent.

But this time it's a challenge for me. I have a lot of questions. A lot of things I need to understand. About where this is going. About the future. Questions I've been meaning to ask. But it can wait. We have a safehouse in town. She'll be there after I make my drop.

After tying up at the dock, we douse the yacht in gasoline and set it ablaze. The first billow of black smoke seeps from the sealed cabin as we head to our separate vehicles.

We share one last look before parting. There's fifty feet between us, but I see a flicker of regret there. Is she changing her mind? But then she's in her car and speeding off. She doesn't slow at the yacht club gate, either. She smashes straight through and disappears with a squeal of tires.

Oh. Shit.

I don't bother confirming what I know. I simply toss the backpack into my car, slam the door shut and sprint for the docks. I'm in the air when the backpack explodes. Shrapnel rips through my thigh before I hit the water. I slide beneath the surface, replaying the audacity of what she has just pulled off in my mind. She is a one of a kind woman.

I come up with a smile. "Atta girl."

As I swim back to shore, my body ablaze with pain that won't subside for days—maybe longer—I decide it's time to pick up a ring. What's the worst that could happen? *She could say no*, I think. But she won't. I'm sure of it. She could have killed me. Twice. But she risked everything to save me—aimed for my shoulder instead of my head, and just now sped away fast enough to warm me.

Most guys would run the other way, change their names and pray to never see her again. Me? I suppose I'm like a male praying mantis—I know she could eat my head off, but I can't resist her. She's worth the risk.

AFTERWORD

This is the only new short story in the bunch. I wrote this in Spring of 2010 when the ITW (International Thriller Writers) announced that their third short story collection, THRILLER 3, would be a series of romantic thrillers. I know, I know, forgive me. My first thought was, "Oh c'mon!" But, I slowly realized this was an interesting challenge. After all, the only difference between a thriller and a romantic thriller is that a romantic relationship is at the center of the story. Thinking back, THE DIDYMUS CONTINGENCY, RAISING THE PAST and without a doubt, KRONOS, hinge upon romantic relationships.

Now, I should mention that at the time of writing this afterword, the ITW has not yet announced the final stories to be included. So if STAR CROSSED KILLERS is accepted, I will be hastily removing it from this collection and whistling an innocent tune. But, with so many amazing, and bestselling authors submitting to the collection and so few spots available (I think just one or two), the odds of being selected are small.

My goal with this story, beyond inclusion in the ITW collection, was to come up with a concept that would 1.) Be considered a romantic thriller (which is the bestselling thriller genre, by the way) and 2.) Not make me feel dirty for writing it. I'm happy with the end result, and I only feel a little bit dirty...but sometimes that's a good thing.

COUNTING SHEEP

One...

Two...

Three...

Once every second, sheep began to materialize in my mind. I could see their fluffy white bodies, black faces and ashen hooves trotting into my imaginary field of vision from the right. With broad, gravity-defying jumps, they leapt a gleaming white, picket fence—the kind you see in history books from the twenty-first century.

Of course, the fact that I even knew what sheep were, being a man of the twenty second century, was a bit of a miracle. My great grandfather had a collection of paper-bound encyclopedias in the basement of his home when he died. I was ten at the time and helped the family clean out the basement where I discovered the collection, from A-Z. It was a world unknown to me, and to the rest of the world.

All of Earth's sheep had gone extinct in recent years. Sheep, it turns out, were cloned to extinction. The perfect sheep had been genetically bred and then cloned, ad infinitum, until all of the world's sheep were identical. All was well and good until a virus that only attacked sheep with a certain genetic flaw sprung up in what was once China. Unfortunately, the original genetically created sheep had this flaw, meaning that all sheep on the planet had this flaw. The virus spread globally within three months, and the world's sheep vanished.

I grew up in a world without lamb chops, wool or mutton. Of course I didn't really miss those things. I never felt or tasted them to know what I was missing.

Thirty-eight…

Thirty-nine…

Forty…

During my childhood sheep research, I came across a passage about counting sheep and how people had actually prescribed the activity as a way to combat sleeplessness.

I was now in a situation to find out for myself.

But sleep wasn't coming easy—even with the sheep.

Every night of my life, as far back as I can remember—pre encyclopedia—I have had a set routine of how to do things before and while I'm in bed. For starters, my teeth have to be brushed. My own bad breath at night, reflecting off a nearby pillow and back into my face, is enough to make me toss and turn. Then the holoshades are

activated. None of this half tint other people use. I need one hun-
dred-percent UV blockage. Then with the shades activated, I sit in
bed for one hour and read, but not on a portoscreen or techno-
deck—the glow from the screens stings my eyes. I read paper books,
and I have to pay a fortune to get them made up.

As soon as the hour of reading is up, I strip down to nothing,
turn on my box-fan and stand in front of the strong breeze, chilling
my body. When I can no longer stand the cold, I jump into bed,
whip the blankets over my body and shuffle my feet together until
I'm warm. And finally, I lie on my stomach, extend my left leg off
the left side of the bed and kick it back and forth until I fall asleep,
usually two hours later.

The worst of it is that at the beginning of this four hour ritual, I
take a sleeping pill that's supposed to knock me out in a half hour.

Ninety-one…

Ninety-two…

Ninety-three…

And now, when it matters most, when I'm being forced to fall
asleep on command, I have none of those things.

Here's what I do have.

A man, whom I've never met before in my life, is holding an el-
derly woman and her granddaughter hostage. His one demand; that
I fall asleep within the next three minutes or he detonates a thermite
grenade strapped to his waist. As I said, I don't know this man, the
old woman or the little girl. Having concluded my four day vacation to the moon, I was walking through the spaceport at Moon-
Hab-3, preparing to depart for Earth. Without warning, the man,

who had somehow made it through security, sprung from the side of a robotic cleaning unit, grabbed the woman and the girl and in a shrill voice, brought attention to his thermite grenade.

Stunned, my legs locked solid and my eyes remained fixated on the explosive device, which looked real enough. Thermite grenades, from what I knew, were used by the military as antitank weaponry, meaning the explosion it created would probably be strong enough to flatten a good portion of the terminal.

When the shock subsided, I scanned the terminal with my eyes and found that every living soul had vacated the area. Just the four of us were left. Then, without warning, and from my perspective, without any goal in mind, he made his demands to me.

"You be asleep," he said in a thick accent I couldn't place. "In three minute. You be asleep!"

"Okay! Okay!" I shouted, terrified that if I didn't comply, he would blow us all up early. When I lay down on the floor, I knew it would be impossible for me to reach slumber.

One hundred forty…

One hundred forty one…

One hundred forty two…

The floor was hard and cold. I had no blankets, no bed to kick my leg off of, no electric hum of the box fan, which I now missed like it was my best friend. There was no book and no time to read if I had access to one. My sleeping pills were packed away in my luggage, and my breath smelled of the sausage and sauerkraut I had for lunch. Worst of all, I was lying beneath a fifty-foot window on the bright side of the moon. All I had was the sheep, and as I reached one hundred sixty, I realized that they were useless.

I'm glad they're extinct!

A thought screeched into my cortex and my eyes opened wide. His demand, "In three minute, you fall asleep," no longer sounded like a demand, but more of a statement. He wasn't telling me what to do. He was telling me what would happen!

Three minutes!

One hundred seventy five...

One hundred seventy six...

One hundred seventy seven...

I knew now that whether or not I fell asleep had no bearing on what this man was going to do. The only change slumber could bring would be that I wouldn't feel so nervous. I looked at the man and watched as his finger depressed a button on the grenade. It blinked *once.*

I miss my box fan.

One hundred seventy eight...

Twice...

I don't want to sleep.

One hundred seventy nine...

Three times...

Useless sheep.

One hundred eighty—

AFTERWORD

Back to insomnia. I wrote this story late at night after failing to fall asleep, and I think my frustration over not sleeping comes through pretty clearly. Perhaps most interesting is that the main character's four-hour sleep routine is mine. While I don't stand in front of a fan and chill myself every night, I have. And my real routine actually involves more steps, and more often than not, fails to achieve the goal of falling asleep before 2am, without resorting to taking a drug.

For the record, I've tried counting sheep. It's incredibly difficult to do, because my imagination is hard to control, but I have tried visualizing the sheep while counting them jumping over a fence. It worked. Once. The fan is a must, even with Ambien. The white noise blocks out most others that would normally set off my sensory disorder, which can, and has (during power outages) defeated the sleep inducing pharmaceutical.

You might be wondering why I don't take Ambien every night. Well, for a month, I did. But like all drugs, Ambien has side effects. Some of them are frightening, especially for people taking the drug nightly as I had been. My doctor failed to mention this to me. While I was sleeping well for the first time in my life, I started feeling this strange energy in my muscles. No matter how much physical activity I did, my body felt like it needed to run. I was constantly stretching, and moving, and feeling manic. One day, when this feeling was particularly intense, I went outside to shoot some hoops. I didn't miss. I normally shoot about 60% on the inside and 30%

from three point range. Not great, but hey, I'm a writer, and soccer is my game. But on this day I was 100% from everywhere. I started taking shots from three point range. Hit them all. I moved further back and hit everything. While this was very cool, it also freaked me out. About fifteen minutes into this, my wife appeared in a window and asked a question. I told her about my strange shooting ability, saw that she doubted me (she's a better shot than I am) and I said, "watch." Without glancing back at the hoop, which was well beyond three point range, I tossed the ball over my head. Swish.

I went off of Ambien that night and hallucinated. Over the next month, I weaned myself off of the drug and now only take it in times of desperation. My basketball skills have returned to normal. As has my sleep, or lack thereof. But I'd rather not sleep than have my mind and body altered by a drug that, had I continued taking it, could have screwed me up in a much less, "I could be a super hero!" kind of way.

*One final note! When I wrote this story, there was no such thing as e-ink, so my vision of the future's e-readers included glaring screens. Alas, I was so short-sighted.

HEARING AID

2067 was the year that dreams came true. It also happened to be my sixty-seventh birthday, and I received a gift—an unbelievable gift of mercy. It took ten years to schedule, clear the red tape and find the right doctors, but I believed it was worth every minute, every dollar Heidi and I dumped into what she called my "Hearing Fund."

I was the second baby born in the new millennium and unlike the first, I came out of the womb stone deaf. They explained to me that when I came out of the womb, I screamed louder than any baby they'd seen before. Of course it wasn't until later that they realized I couldn't hear the sound of my own voice, so I hollered like a person wearing headphones, not that I know what that's like.

But I would.

The treatment I underwent was new and like the day I was born, I was second in line. The first to try it turned out to be less healthy than the first millennium baby, though. Doctors said he had some kind of disorder, something wrong in his mind that the operation triggered. They told me that what happened to him was an accident; that it had nothing to do with the procedure. I believed them, but I've never heard of suicide referred to as an accident.

When I entered the hospital, I felt a feeling of tranquility wash over me. I got the same feeling every time I entered the lobby. The sun's rays streamed in through the large windows that lined the entrance way and the left side of the long hallway, warming my skin. The French vanilla air freshener tickled my nose set my mouth to salivating. It was fairly busy, I guess. Some people seemed to be in a hurry, but nothing urgent and we only waited in line ten minutes before getting to the desk. The woman behind the reception desk punched my name in the computer, read the information on the holographic projection and gave me a bright smile.

"Right this way," she said, and then quickly looked embarrassed. "Sorry," she signed. "I'm forgetful."

"It's okay," I signed. "I can read lips."

The woman nodded, looking relieved, and led me down a hallway while everyone else in the waiting room was left behind. Seemed patients for ear surgery got the royal treatment around this place.

A half hour later I found myself lying on a cold table, wearing some kind of fancy underwear and feeling like a half-naked old fool. Of course, I still thought the humiliation was worth it. I had tried every hearing aid in existence, but nothing worked. The doctors told me some technical jargon about why my ears didn't work, but the plain and simple of it was actually just that: plain and simple. One thingy wasn't connected to another thingy. Reconnect them and presto, I would hear. Of course, the doctors didn't like my simplified explanation much, but it helped me understand what went on inside my cranium.

Then they explained the really hard part. Normally, in the past, when people who were born deaf or who went deaf regained their hearing, it took them years to understand what they were hearing, to differentiate a cow from a car and a word from a fart. Plus they had to learn language, how to use their own voice, all things usually done when they're children and the brain is much more adaptive. Life expectancy wavered somewhere around one hundred twenty years those days so I still had almost another sixty to go, but I was old. I can admit that much. Learning new things no longer felt doable.

No problem, the doctors told me when I expressed my concern. The second part of the procedure took care of the learning aspect, too. Some science geniuses figured out what part of the brain controls and interprets sounds, language, yadda, yadda, and figured out how to transplant understanding into a mind that had none. I would wake up and not just understand the English language, but I would be able to speak it perfectly. I would be able to enjoy a symphony orchestra. Hell, they even gave me the option to understand and speak other languages. I chose Spanish. Those little Spanish lolitas still got me worked up. I may have been old, but I wasn't dead.

The last thing I saw before passing out on the table was a smiling doctor signing to me, "Try to relax. Everything's going to be fine."

When I woke up, I felt a familiar cushion beneath my body—my bed, at home. And it was still quiet...not that I had any idea what hearing would sound like...

Or did I? A new sensation began to tickle my mind...something I couldn't quite place. A hiss, I thought.

I reached up and felt my ears. Cotton wrappings tightly covered them. Before I could undo the wrapping, I saw a note on the bedside table. I read it quickly:

Peter,

Doctors say everything went fine. Sorry I couldn't be there with you for the operation or when you wake up, but they have me working extra hours to cover the war. I left something playing for you on the holo-station, should be a real treat. Love you.

–   Heidi.

I smiled. At twenty years my junior, I constantly felt amazed that Heidi could love me so deeply. She was a correspondent at one of the local channels and covered America's latest war—the Australian's had invaded Japan. Two of our favorite friends picked a fight with each other and we were forced to choose sides. Ironic we chose the nation that dealt us one of our worst defeats at Pearl Harbor way back when.

My mind returned to the note. Something was playing on the holo-station. I sat up on the side of the bed and got my bearings. Everything felt normal. I stood and still felt fine. That's when I unwrapped the headdress that covered my ears.

I did my best to ignore any sounds sneaking through as I unwrapped the headdress, but the light scraping sound of fabric on hair seemed loud in my ears. Even harder to ignore was the fact that I *knew* it was the sound that fabric made when it rubbed against hair. Amazing.

The fabric came away from my ears with a final whoosh of sound and then it struck me. The second sound I'd ever heard in my life wafted through the air like a beautiful melody. I knew right away that it was a bird...a chickadee. The sounds came from the holo-station. But I heard more...wind...rustling trees...leaves...nature.

I began to cry and let out a little sob. Then I gasped at the sound of my own voice. It was deep, powerful even. I walked to the mirror and spoke to myself, "Hello Peter. How's it going? Fine. How about you? Hell! I can hear!"

I began to wonder what else there made noise. I walked to the holo-station and turned it off. Silence replaced the birds and wind. But I could hear something... A whistle. A repeating whistle that coincided with every breath I took. I realized that my stuffy nose created a whistle when air rushed past the blockage. Fascinating, but how many times had this happened in the past without my knowledge? The thought of my whistling nose entertaining the people around me became an embarrassing image, and I pushed it from my mind. I headed to the bathroom and blew my nose, which was extremely loud. I flushed the toilet, ran the water in the sink and in the tub and listened to the creak in the medicine cabinet's hinges.

A boisterous, repeating gong rang out from the living room and I ran to investigate. I stopped in front of Heidi's grandfather clock. I had no idea that thing made noise! Then I saw the time. Twelve noon. Heidi was on at noon! I'd watched her almost every day since the day we got married, and I read her lips with every newscast, but today I would hear her for the first time.

I leapt into my leather recliner and noticed it crinkled and flexed loudly underneath my body as I adjusted. I stopped moving, hoping the noise would go away. It did. I looked around for the remote and saw it on the floor, five feet out. Damn. Then it occurred to me that most holo-stations were voice activated! We only had a remote because I had no voice, but I did now. "On, please," I said, mimicking the words I saw Heidi speak to the holo-station in the past. "Channel Twelve news."

The holographic, three-dimensional images flashed into the air in the middle of the room. The news show started and the familiar images of country towns, the big city and the news anchors flashed before my eyes. But there was music, too; powerful sounds that made me feel a sense of urgency.

I sat with rapt attention, but I burst out laughing when Heidi appeared in front of me, crystal clear, like she was sitting across from me. It wasn't the image that brought me so much joy; it was when she spoke, "Good Afternoon, Boston. I'm Heidi Leonard, and this is the news at noon."

Heidi continued to speak, and I paid attention to every syllable. "Today in the war with Australia we had a stunning victory, as the First Fleet pushed the Australian forces past the southern tip of New Zealand." Her voice was soothing...like the angel I knew her to be. I had a sudden urge to use the bathroom, but remained stuck to the chair, intent on hearing every word of Heidi's broadcast. "On the mainland of New Zealand, the fierce fighting between the coalition of Japanese and American forces are still fighting valiantly against the entrenched Australians. We go now, live to our woman in the field, Tyler Genson."

The image changed to that of a grassy battlefield—the kind I had seen on the news before, since the war started six months ago. "Thank you, Heidi..." Tyler was a young lady who I'd met twice before and who always exuded confidence to me. But now I heard her voice...full of nervousness and tension, hidden behind her stoic face. She continued talking, but I no longer heard the words. High-pitched whistles zoomed through my ears. Explosions. Shouting voices. Tyler ducked as something loud and massive struck the ground nearby, launching dirt through the shot. As the vibrations from the explosion faded, the screams of men and woman boomed from the holo-station's surround-sound speaker system. Then machine-gun fire. Screeching rockets. Pounding helicopters.

Chaos!

I'd seen pictures like this before, but hearing it...I began to panic. I covered my ears with my hands and shouted at the holographic image of Tyler, "Get out of there! Run! Tyler, get the hell out of there!"

But she didn't run, she kept right on reporting what everyone could see and hear for themselves. "Off! Now!" The holo-station blinked off. My mind swirled with a mass of confused thoughts. I needed some air.

"Open," I said to the window, knowing it would work. The

window slid open sideways, and the cool harbor air hit me, calming me. Then the noise struck. A cacophony of grinding metal, loud engines, shouting people and squawking billboards assaulted my healed ears. The view I had enjoyed so much, the shimmering ocean, which my apartment building hovered above on tall pylons, the flying cars, which had become so popular in the past twenty years, the hundreds of skyscrapers that lined the mainland and spilled out into the harbor, like a partially sunken city...had become chaotic, tense, rushed and angry.

My breathing began to speed. My heart pumped so fast I could hear the damn blood slamming past my ears.

I needed...I needed something to eat.

"Close!" The window slid shut.

I walked to the kitchen and opened the fridge. Nothing. How long was I asleep for and why didn't Heidi get any food? I slammed the fridge and the loud bang made me jump. I opened a cupboard and a single box of Wheat Tasties sat there. I picked it up. "Thank you for trying Wheat Tasties!" the box said.

I dropped the Wheat Tasties on the floor and stared at the box...waiting.... Nothing happened. I moved away. "You're not done are you? Everyone needs to eat their Wheat Tasties!"

I jumped back.

"Thank you for trying Wheat Tasties! And next time you're out, pick up a box of our new Pesto Wheat Tasties. Remember, Wheat Tasties are what's good in life!"

I turned from the box and ran out of the apartment.

Less than a minute later I spilled out onto the sidewalk, which was a taut wire mesh, allowing pedestrians to see the waves crash against the pylons that supported the buildings above the water. I had always wondered what those waves would sound like, but now all I could hear were the new cars zipping past overhead, the old cars roaring past on the grated streets and a chaotic cauldron of human voices that made no sense at all!

I could make out words here and there, and I knew that this was what thousands of human voices all talking at once sounded like, but it was unbearable. I blocked my ears with my hands, which drew a few odd glances. I then noticed who everyone was talking to—no one at all. Everyone on the sidewalks had small devices attached to their cheeks...cell phones. Everyone carried on conversations, but to no one physically present.

My mind spun. This felt unbearable. There had to be a volume control, some way to tune out the noises. But I knew otherwise. Hearing was hearing, and noise was noise. Still feeling hungry, I ducked into the small grocery store built into the outside corner of my building. Food shopping always relaxed me.

I walked through the first aisle as usual, heading for the chocolate ice cream. That was when all hell broke loose.

"Try Ameriwhip today!"

"Have you had a V18 today?"

"Do people tell you you're overweight?"

"Uh-oh! Somebody looks sad! You need a honey ham!"

I began running down the aisle as every product I passed assaulted me with sales pitches and personal living tips. That's when I heard it. "Thank you for trying Wheat Tasties!" I slid to a stop and looked at a product display of Wheat Tasties, all varieties. As though sensing I had stopped, they all sang out in unison, "Everyone needs to eat their Wheat Tasties! Buy us! C'mon! You can eat us all! We're good for you."

My eyes widened while my forehead furrowed deeply. I turned and ran out of the store, having made it only fifteen feet inside.

I covered my ears with my hands and made a beeline for the hospital, knowing that someone there would be able to help. At least it would be quieter.

Five minutes later I arrived at the hospital and entered the first set of sliding doors. The first set of doors closed behind me as I approached the second. All I could hear was the hiss of the air conditioning vents. Better already.

I could see through the glass of the second set of doors and the hospital waiting room looked the same as usual, busy, yet peaceful. The sun still streamed through windows and it was quiet.

The second set of doors slid open and I nearly fell backwards when the noise flooded across the foyer. People screamed, some in pain. Doctors shouted for help. The people in line griped about the wait. "Doctor Sullivan," a voice, like that of God Himself, boomed through the air. My mind told me it was an intercom system. "Doctor Sullivan, you're needed in the O.R. stat. Doctor Sullivan, you are needed in the O.R. stat."

Chaos!

Everything I had enjoyed, even loved before, had been perverted. Even the mundane pleasure of Wheat Tasties had become the Devil's work! I stumbled backward, back onto the street, when a car honked loudly. A baby screamed for who knows what. A man cleared his juicy throat and spat his mucus near my feet. I ran back to the apartment, ears covered, and formulated a plan.

I knew what I had to do.

I entered the apartment and was immediately greeted. "Thank you for trying Wheat Tasties! And next time you're out, pick up...a box...of...our ne—" I stomped on the box until it shut up.

I burst into the bedroom and headed for my dresser. Two rows of underwear back and one to the right...there it was. I pulled the gun out from the drawer and checked the chamber—still loaded. Guns were severely illegal, but I didn't feel safe without it. Not even Heidi knew I had the thing.

I stood nervously, holding the gun in my hand with my finger on the trigger. This was going to hurt like hell, and I'd be screwed for life if I somehow messed this up. But it was the only way to make it stop. The noise! The chaos had to end.

As I held the cold gun against my head, listening to the silence of my apartment, I had second thoughts. But I knew I couldn't stay hidden away inside forever. I couldn't stop going to the store for chocolate ice cream. I couldn't stop watching Heidi on the holo-station. I couldn't stop enjoying the breeze, the view, the ocean smell from my window. But I could stop it all, with one or two pulls of the trigger. And no one would hear a thing. The padded walls of this apartment that kept the outside noise at bay would keep the inside noise from escaping.

I held my breath and let my index finger squeeze.

The last sound I heard was the loudest, most horrific bang that existed. After that, everything went black.

Four hours later, Heidi walked in the door. "Hey, hon! How are you doing? What do you think of my voice?"

Her excitement was tangible and for the first time, I felt bad about what I did. When I woke up the first time, I placed the gun next to my other ear, maybe an inch from my head, pointed it at my pillow and pulled the trigger again before I remembered how much it would hurt. After waking up the second time, I quickly incinerated the bloody sheet I had put beneath me, in case I bled, which turned out to be good thinking on my part. Then I incinerated my pillow, which served to slow down the bullets. After that, I put the dented cookie sheet, which actually stopped the bullets before they could put holes in the wall, in the dumpster shoot. Heidi didn't cook anyway. She'd never miss it. Ten minutes later, my face was cleaned up and I was looking out the window, enjoying the view, smelling the air, feeling the wind on my face, and hearing absolutely nothing.

"It's beautiful," I signed. "Too bad I can't hear it."

She looked like she might cry, but managed to keep her reporter game face. "Are you okay?"

"I'm fine," I signed.

"Did you see the doctor?"

I nodded and signed, "Nothing they can do. Something wrong with the way my mind works."

"I'm sorry," she said.

"Don't be," I signed. "I think I'm happier this way."

AFTERWORD

This story is a response to two things that have begun to annoy me, and most people—noise pollution and advertising. I wrote this story after living in Los Angles for a few years. There is more advertising and noise in LA than anywhere I've been or suspect I'll ever be, until I visit Tokyo (watching Godzilla in a Tokyo theater is on my list of things to do before I die). There were times in LA, when I longed for silence, when I wished for the glut of advertising to fade. That frustration is at the core of the story.

But the specific inspiration came from an article in Popular Science. It discussed facial-recognition software being utilized in mall advertisements. The signs could determine that the person walking past was a young man, or an old woman, and display a targeted ad. As a person who markets books all the time, I see the money-making value of the system. As a human being, I want to say, "Get out of my brain!" It's too much. And I know it's not the end. As TV advertisements lose their grip on people and we train ourselves to ignore Web-ads (I'm already a pro at this), people with something to sell will find new ways to attract consumers' attention. I have no doubt that targeted audio will find its way to the grocerystore. It's already hard to walk through a toy store and not have several of the toys call out to you. It's the future baby! And when it arrives, you may wish to be deaf, too.

DARK SEED OF THE MOON

The job was simple.

All I had to do was keep the engines running for a trip to the moon and back. Should have gone as smooth as a hairless cat.

Should have.

Next time I'm tempted to think something should go a certain way, I'll remember this trip and then kick myself repeatedly until I squeal. You see, I tend to have a big mouth, and sitting alone in an engine room with nothing to irritate me other than the monotonous hum of the engines, I tend to have very few opportunities to spout off what comes to my mind. Sometimes the words come out of my mouth just as the thought that created them slams into my head. The results aren't always pretty.

"The port side thruster seems a little sticky. We're drifting .005 degrees to starboard with every thrust. See if you can straighten it out." It was the first time this captain had visited the engine room. It was the first time he had asked me to do anything at all. My response was less than professional.

I explained that a .005 degree drift was not only insignificant, but the fact that he had come to the engine room in person to tell me about it was ridiculous.

I was just getting warmed up.

With a loud voice, I declared that if we were traveling to Alpha Centauri, a .005 degree drift would put us way off course, perhaps by a million miles or so, but on a trip from Earth to the moon, .005 degrees was like forgetting to trim a few hairs on a beard. No one would notice.

When I was finally done ranting, the captain chuckled, called me some sort of name—can't remember what it was—and then declared that I'd be lucky to find work at the San Fran Space Port. There goes another port... Only three left in the country that don't have me on the blacklist. I must have turned bright red, because he said something insulting about my face, laughed loudly and then called me a drunk.

I'm a loudmouth. I'll concede that. Sometimes I can be downright obnoxious. But I'm not a drunk. My father was a drunk and a bastard, with tendency to whip children with metal objects. Even before the thought entered my mind, my body had already reacted, and I was only starting to understand what happened when I realized the captain was on the grated floor of the engine room, rubbing his jaw.

Been three hours since then and I'm on cleanup duty—for the rest of the trip. Glad we're just going to the moon. One day there, one day stay and one day back. As long as nothing spills, I'll just be sitting on my rump, just like always, only now I'm sitting in my closet-sized quarters, reading a novel and waiting for something to spill. I should slug captains more often.

"Simon, cleanup in cargo bay 2-C," the first-mate's voice booms over the intercom. I nearly fall from my bunk as his shrill voice wrenches me from a graphic sex scene in which the author took an entire paragraph to describe the woman's breasts.

"And do a good job," the captain adds. "Or we'll leave you at the Dark Crater colony after we make this delivery." Apparently, the captain is looking for me to straighten his jaw with a left hook. Probably a good thing he's choosing to use the intercom this time.

I work my way through the cramped, gray hallways, which smell like mildew, and slide into cargo bay 2-C. The odor hits me first, like fleshy copper. The stench is so pungent and putrid that I cup my hands over my mouth and hold down the bile rising in my throat. The room is so thick with the stuff that I can taste it…which gives me pause.

Familiarity causes the hairs on my legs to bristle.

My forehead wrinkles as I move forward, looking for the spill. A growing sense of dread that makes me want to hit the head before continuing, surges through my guts. But I push on, past the oxygen tanks and cargo crates filled with medical supplies.

I freeze.

Before taking this job I glanced at the cargo manifest and saw the

first few items listed (medical supplies mostly), and then looked at
the location. I saw the word "moon" and signed up. Most trips to
the moon were quick, high paying and relatively easy. The captain's
words finally register in my cortex. He had said, "Dark Crater colony." Lord knows I wouldn't have signed up for a Dark Crater drop.

Rumors ran high when it came to the Dark Crater colony. As
one of the first colonies to be set up independently of any Earth
government, the only way to visit the Dark Crater colony was by
invitation or to make cargo drops, and even then, most cargo crews
were hand-picked by the colony itself—I had been a last-minute
replacement.

Damn.

Damn. Damn. Damn.

I take a deep breath and the sour smell and taste enters my
mouth again. I'm thrown into a coughing fit that burns inside my
chest like my lungs are being ripped at by a feral cat. I fall to one
knee and realize I need to see it for myself, confirm the fear itching
at the back of my skull.

I head toward the back of the room where a wall of barrels are
stacked five deep, four high and thirty across. A puddle sits on the
floor ten feet to my right, but I don't see a leak. With my arm over
my mouth and nose, I head for the spill and stop two feet away,
staring at the crimson liquid.

Following the spill to the nearest barrel, I read the label, which is
written in bold text and accompanied by several warning and haz-
mat emblems. My chest pounds as theories race through my mind.
Maybe there's some kind of medical emergency? A disaster of some

kind. The need might be high if there was a large number of injured. Walking quickly along the line of barrels, I read the labels on each one.

All the same.

I can hear a rushing sound behind my eardrums and I've all but forgotten about the smell. I rush to the computer console next to the door and access the cargo manifest, reading it in more detail this time. The first page looks normal—construction supplies, medical supplies—but no food. Most colonies have working greenhouses and interior farms that provide some food, but imported Earth food is usually the number one cargo item. I scan forward to the next page, expecting to see a long list of food items.

After ten lines of text scroll by, my finger freezes on the keyboard and the list continues to scroll down. For a minute straight, the long list of barreled cargo scrolls past my stunned eyes. There's no food at all...or is there?

A few others have gone to the crater and back and told horror stories about what they saw there, the kind of folks that live there. Most are written off as jealous blue-collar workers, envious of the rich who can afford to live on a colony with a never-ending perfect view of the stars. But now I think the rumors might be true, which makes the rest of this hand-picked crew highly suspect and me a severely endangered loudmouth.

I scan the list again, confirming that this nightmare is reality. I read the lines over and over:

Plasma – 15 gallons – A Positive

Plasma – 15 gallons – B Negative

Plasma – 15 gallons – O Negative

Plasma – 15 gallons – A Positive

The list goes on for pages, thousands of gallons, all containing the same thing.

Blood.

My eyes sting with perspiration. I didn't bother cleaning up the puddle of blood. Screw that. My thoughts were now on how I could get back to SanFran with my life intact. I beg my mind for some kind of answer, some kind of plan, but the chaotic swirl of thoughts within my brainpan fails to congeal into anything useful. Tradition dictates specific ways to defend yourself in a situation like this, but we're on a damned spaceship approaching a crater at the north pole of the moon. I don't have access to anything that might work.

A voice form the intercom slams into my eardrum. "Making final approach. All hands report to the docking bay for transport of goods and one day's leave."

A pain throbs in my throat, but fades quickly when a glimmer of hope dawns on me, as though a message from God. I didn't clean up the spill. I disobeyed orders, again. Surely they will confine me to quarters while everyone disembarks for a day of frivolity. I pound up the metal floor toward my quarters, hoping the order to stay put will come before I get there.

As I enter the last in a maze of hallways and make a beeline for my quarters, a body moves out of the darkness from around a corner. I jump back, gripping my chest.

The captain.

The *smiling* captain. "Good job with the cleanup, Simon. Try not to hit me again and I might just keep you around."

"Thanks," I say, though Lord knows I just want to hit the guy again and get confined to quarters, but I'm afraid of what else might happen.

"This your first visit to the Dark Crater colony?" the captain asks.

I nod, nervously wringing my hands together.

"Good…good… I think you'll be happily surprised with the accommodations." The captain places his hand on my shoulder, and I can feel him gently directing me toward the docking bay.

Damn. Damn. Damn.

The fact that the internal temperature of the dimly lit, lunar docking bay is hanging somewhere around fifty degrees isn't doing wonders to calm my nerves. The lighting is a real hoot too. My eyes start to adjust to the nearly pitch-black surroundings. I can hear the breathing of the cargo ship's crew, moving around me, bumping into me, and I expect to be torn to shreds at any moment. I'm so tense that when the cargo-bay doors open with a clang, it takes all of my remaining courage to keep from screaming like a B-movie actress.

The doors split in the middle and slide away in either direction, allowing a red light to spill into the room. The cargo bay glows like the fiery embers of Hades, and a chill runs across my back. A slew of profanities cross my mind and nearly escape my lips, but for the first time in a long time, my mind is quicker on the draw than my tongue and I hold it. I seriously doubt that the cargo crew, captain or the massive Dark Crater colony workers now entering the cargo bay would appreciate what I have to say.

Fourteen strapping men dressed in jet-black jumpsuits enter the bay, approach the captain and silently look over the manifest. The largest of the beefcakes nods to the captain and the men set to work unloading the barrels of blood. My body begins to move. Helping unload is the only action that seems like it won't raise suspicion now. Before I've taken two steps, a hand on my shoulder locks my feet to the solid metal floor.

Eyes clenched and sure that death is looming just behind me, I turn around to face it like a man.

"Simon, right?"

The voice is soft, feminine and so overtly friendly that I sigh with relief before taking in the face of an angel. Standing at five foot six, just a few shorter than myself, I look into the deep brown eyes of a woman, whose skin glows pink in the red light. She smiles at me wide, revealing her perfect, gleaming teeth.

"Yeah…yeah, I'm Simon." It's all I can manage.

Playing with her straight, shiny black hair, she says, "I'm Rachel. I'm kind of the welcoming committee to folks who haven't been to the DCC, and it's a rule here that first time visitors get special treatment."

"But…but I'm on the clock." Even with the feeling of impending doom, I'm still worried about salvaging my failing career. Stupid.

"It's all been arranged with your captain," she says, which I doubt is true, so I look over at the old man. He sees me, gives a nod and waives me away.

What the hell.

"You see," Rachel says with a perky smile, "We do this with all first timers, the captain included...twenty seven years ago if I remember correctly."

"Somehow I don't think you were around twenty-seven years ago," I say without thinking.

"You'd be surprised," Rachel says in reply. "Living in the crater, out of the sun, has a way of keeping people looking young."

Her words feed the pattern that started to develop in my mind with the spilled blood, but her voice keeps me from panicking. She takes my hand and pulls me toward the exit. "C'mon, let me give you the tour."

We walked and talked for twenty minutes as she showed me what looked like your standard vacation colony, except that the whole place was lit only with red lights. Quarters were spacious and nicely decorated with fresh flowers and authentic paintings by some of Earth's best—some she explained, had been the property of some of the colony's patrons for hundreds of years. The few people we did pass nodded politely, smiled and continued on their way.

Now we're standing outside a large door and I'm feeling nervous about what might be on the other side. Rachel pushes a button next to the door and it slides open. I step in and gasp. Rachel stifles a giggle, but I hardly notice. The site before me is unlike anything I've ever seen in my life.

Craning my head up for the best view, I stumble toward the center of the room, keeping my eyes glued on the view. Above my head is a clear dome that provides the perfect view of the stars. It's breathtaking. I've spent the majority of my life floating around in space, but most times within the windowless bowels of an engine room. The few times I got a peek out the window of a cargo cruiser pale in comparison to this. I felt like I was floating free among the stars.

"This is the star room. How does it make you feel?" Rachel asks.

I look in her eyes and she smiles, waiting for an answer. My eyes return to the view. "Free," I say.

"That's the idea," she said. "That's what DCC was created for, freedom."

"From what?" I ask, eyes bouncing from one pinpoint of light to another.

"From oppression," she says.

"There's no oppression on Earth anymore."

"There is for us."

I look at her again. "I doubt it…you're beautiful."

Damn. Damn. Damn.

There goes my mouth again.

"Sorry, I—"

"I'm flattered," she says.

Amazing.

"Some of us have been here so long that we're just another face," she says, eyes glimmering.

I decide to take a risk. "I don't think you could ever be just another face to me. Not in a million years." Not exactly eloquent, but I think I got the message across.

She smiles wide, obviously flattered. "I'll keep that in mind."

My vision is drawn back toward the ceiling. I point at one of the glowing pinpoints of light. "What's that one?"

"Mars," she says. "You can tell because of its red color."

I can't resist. "Speaking of red, what's with all the red lights?"

"Living in the crater makes most light seem abnormally bright. After you've been here for a few years, anything brighter than what you see now might give you a migraine."

"Too bad I'm only here for a day," I say.

She smiles at me with squinting eyes that say she knows something I don't. My concerns about this place rush back into my mind all at once, and I immediately forget that this beautiful woman has been flirting with me. "So," I say with a quiver in my voice that even I can hear, "You never told me why you're oppressed on Earth."

She looks at the floor and then returns her gaze to me. It's penetrating. "I'm not supposed to tell you. But you seem…different, like you might understand."

I nod, doubting that what she's saying is true while trying to think of a way back through the colony, onto the cargo ship and off the moon.

"We're vampires."

My thoughts come to a crashing halt. She just came out and said it? Just like that? We're vampires? Nothing creepy. No blah blah, I want to suck your blood. Then I notice how anxious she looks, how afraid of me, what I might say. "Vampires?"

She seems relieved by my one word reaction. She sighs and says, "Vampires…We drink human blood for sustenance. We grow ill from sunlight and die painfully if exposure is prolonged. That's why we live here, in the crater. Because of its placement on the North Pole, we are always concealed in shadow. We live for hundreds, sometimes thousands of years…I'm three hundred and fifty seven years old."

Just when I think I'm at a loss for words, my mouth begins forming syllables and then sentences. "What about garlic, crucifixes, wooden stakes, mirror reflections, that stuff?"

That's where myth and fact go their separate ways," she says with a smile. "We're not undead, just a mutation of normal people. In our lives, our work, beliefs, hobbies, we're just as human as you."

I find the mass of new thoughts and ideas entering my mind too confusing and surprising. This isn't anything like I pictured it would be. This woman, this vampire, has managed to put me at ease even with my career going up in flames, even after seeing with the spilled blood and having thoughts of being eaten alive. I find myself thinking she's the most extraordinary creature I've laid eyes on. Then I realize that, in fact, she is. I smile at her and can't believe the words are coming from my mouth even as I speak them. "From what I've seen, you're more human than most people I've ever met on Earth."

She stands silent. Stunned.

Her hand flies to her face, covering her mouth. "Oh my God," she says.

"What?"

Her eyes look afraid, but not for herself. Before I can think on it any more, the fear is wiped form her face and she says, "Come with me." She takes me by the hand and leads me quickly out of the star-filled room. Apparently, the tour is over. But I'm not sure I want to find out what happens next.

Rachel leads me through a series of hallways, pulling on my wrist and hiding me from passersby. The urgency in her voice as she tells me to follow keeps me moving, but the feeling that this is some kind of elaborate trap has yet to leave my mind. She is a vampire after all. Not that I've known any other vampires…but still.

We stop in front of an unlabeled door and Rachel glances in either direction, looking for God knows what. She places her hand on a flat panel to the side of the door, which glows red when her hand touches its surface. The doors slides open and Rachel pulls me inside.

Upon entering the room I begin to sweat. Not because of the running through the hallways, or because the air is warm—it's not—but because I'm overcome by two simultaneous emotions, both of which can promote overactive sweat glands, extreme fear and excitement. Some people live for the combination of fear and excitement, but I tend to avoid both on a daily basis.

I look around the bedroom. The bed is lavishly decorated with fine violet sheets…looks like silk. Pieces of fine art, accentuated by ornately carved gold frames, hang on the walls. But what stands out most are the roses. They're everywhere. Every flat surface in the room contains a crystal vase overflowing with red roses, which glow even redder in the ruby light.

Normally, in a situation like this, my clothes would be on the floor in a quickly formed pile by now. But this isn't normal. The door closes behind me.

I feel a cold hand grasp my wrist and I gasp.

I turn toward Rachel, and I understand what she wants.

"Why?" I ask.

"You're in danger."

"I figured that."

"They're going to kill you."

"Why the tour?"

"To distract you…they knew you'd be suspicious of the air and lighting."

"But you told me…you know, that you're vampires."

"I know."

"Why?"

"Because I've been stuck here for almost a hundred years and in that time no one has paid any attention to me like you have. Remember, I'm not dead. I'm not undead. I still have needs and desires. I've been alone for three lifetimes."

If I'm falling for a trap, I don't care. "But you're… you're beautiful."

"I'm a misfit among outcasts." She looks at the floor. I believe this is hard for her. "I've never hunted—never killed a human being before."

Inwardly, I sigh with relief. "That's a bad thing?"

She nods. "It's part of our history that isn't fiction. I think it's disgusting…killing those weaker than us, and it's why you're here."

I hold my breath. "When a new vampire is brought to DCC they're initiated by a hunt. You're supposed to be the prey."

"When?" I ask.

"Tomorrow."

My head lowers to the floor. I'm on a space station filled with vampires, in the bedroom of one of them, and I've got no way home. Not one of my brighter moments. "What are you planning to do with me?"

She sits on the bed and stretches, pushing her chest out. She looks at me with eyes that replace anything she could have said.

"How's that going to help?"

"Trust me," she says.

Trust her? Trust a vampire? I can barely trust that this is real.

Trust or no trust, my future looks grim. I've never been a glass-half-empty kind of guy though. I decide to trust…at least for the night. I take her head in my hands, feel the softness of her cheeks and fall into bed.

I wake up the next morning, at least I think its morning, and look at the stranger lying next to me. Her slender, curved body is hugged closely by the thin purple sheets. I follow the rise and dip of her hip, up across her torso to her exposed arm and finally stop at her closed eyes. She's sensational.

I hold my breath when I remember some of the old vampire stories, which she claims are fiction. I recall certain vampires having the ability to seduce members of the opposite sex with ease, only to rip open the victim's neck and drink their blood.

I slide out of bed and just for the hell of it, make a cross with my fingers and point it in her direction. Nothing happens.

I turn to a mirror across the room, which is lined by red roses. Bending my neck in either direction, I inspect my jugular for even the slightest wound. I discover nothing, but I am discovered.

"Don't worry," Rachel says. "If I wanted to drink your blood, you'd be dead."

"Isn't that how other people become vampires?"

She smiles her comforting smile. "No…becoming a vampire, if you're not born a vampire is a much more pleasant experience."

I feel my eyebrows furrow deeply. "Then how—"

My question is cut short by a knock at the door.

Rachel's eyes go wide, and my chest begins to pound. I forgot where I was, why I was here.

"Over there," she says, pointing to a purple drape, hanging from one wall.

I understand what she wants and quickly duck behind the flowing wall covering. I feel invisible behind the drape, but my nerves are shot. I'm like a nervous child hiding during a game of hide and seek. An overwhelming sense of having to use the bathroom makes my pelvis muscles tighten. As the door whooshes open I hold my breath, clench my buttocks and open my ears.

"Where's the prey?" I hear a man with a deep voice ask. "He's not in his quarters."

"I brought him to one of the luxury suites to ease his nerves. He was very suspicious. I knew you wanted him to be unaware... I should have told you. My apologies."

She's a quick thinker. That's good.

"You were wise to move him. Are you sure you don't want to partake in the hunt? You have so much potential. Your talents are being wasted."

"I am...content with my place here," Rachel says.

"Very well. It is, after all, your choice."

I hear feet begin to shuffle away, then stop. "Rachel, would you be so kind as to fetch the prey and bring him to the dining room. We want him feeling comfortable in your hands, now don't we?"

"Of course."

The feet clomp away and the door slides shut. I nearly scream as Rachel pulls the drapes away, but manage to hold my voice in my throat. She sees my reaction and holds her finger to her lips, urging me to stay silent. I nod reassuringly and say, "Do you have a bathroom?"

Rachel chuckles playfully at my question, which was apparently the last thing she expected.

After using the bathroom, the door to which seamlessly molded into the bedroom wall, I come out, feeling more relaxed and very energized. In fact, I feel better than ever. She's already dressed—all black, but something looks different. She looks ready for action. "You guys pump this place full of extra O2? I feel great."

She doesn't seem surprised. "Really? Have you looked in the mirror?"

"Just at my neck...why?"

"Look," she says with a smirk.

I walk to the full mirror and look at my mug...looks the same to me, a little flush maybe, but otherwise the same. Rachel walks up behind me and wraps her arms around my torso, caressing my chest with her hands.

"Lower," she says.

I lift my shirt slowly and stop half way up, admiring the six pack that is chiseled where my chubby ponch used to rest. I lift the shirt higher and see a pair of pectoral muscles that I've never seen before. Rachel's face smiles at me through the mirror. "What did you do?"

"You're one of us now," she says.

My mind spins with all the possibilities and ramifications of what she's just told me. I'm a vampire... I'm a damn vampire! "How?" I ask while reinspecting my neck for bite marks.

She brushes my hands away from my neck and laughs gently. "I told you, that's not how it works."

I spin towards, feeling angry, fearful...strong. "Then how?"

"Last night."

"Last night, what?"

She smiles and glances down at my crotch. My eyes go wide. "You didn't bite me down there!"

She laughs out loud and covers her mouth. "You became a vampire while we were making love. The change is transferred like a sexually transmitted disease…only you're not diseased, or un-dead…" She leans in close to my ear and whispers. "You're immortal."

Something inside me likes the sound of that. I step back. "What else?"

"The transferring of vampiric energy fades after every time a vampire makes love to a normal human. Each new lover is given less and less and eventually, perhaps after thirty or so human lovers, the vampire can no longer spread the change. Each of the new vampires are given the traits of all vampires, born a vampire or changed, all the traits are the same, only in different degrees. The first human lover of a vampire is given the powers of a vampire born. Enhanced speed, strength, healing and longevity are all transferred. But with the change comes a dependence on human blood for sustaining our lives, not a thirst mind you, dependence. I personally take my blood through injections. I can't stand to drink it straight. Any more questions?"

"Just one…how many lovers did you have before me. Human, I mean."

She smiles her perfect smile again. "None."

"Then I'm as strong as any vampire?"

She nods. "For at least the next month or so, then you'll need some blood."

"And I don't have to drink it?"

"No."

I smile wide, hardly believing what's happening, but loving every second of my newfound lease on life and superhuman powers. Then

I remember that the other vampires at DCC want to kill me and drink my blood. "We need to get out of here."

"The path to the docking bay should be clear. I have my own ship."

I nod and she opens the door, looks both ways and waves for me to follow her.

Minutes passed and the hallways appeared to be deserted.

"How much further?" I ask, as we round a corner.

"Through the star room and straight through for another hundred meters. My ship is docked next to the bay you came in."

I nod and we head through the doors into the star room. As we pass through, I'm captivated again, and my eyes are drawn to the stars above. As I take in the lights, a darkness slides across the ceiling, obscuring the stars as it moves. My muscles tense, and I feel a sense which I've never felt before, but which I understand immediately.

The shadow descends.

"Look out!" I push Rachel to the side and the dark blur lands where she was standing.

A man, perhaps six foot five and thick, stands in front of me. His shirtless torso ripples with massive muscles the likes of which I've never seen. His hair is stark white, like an albino, but his eyes are dark, almost black.

"I'm impressed. You have fast reflexes for a human." He doesn't know. "Perhaps you will survive the hunt longer than expected."

I stand speechless, not knowing who this is or how powerful he is. I don't dare act or speak.

The man turns his head toward Rachel. "And where are you going?"

Rachel remains silent, staring at the floor.

With a speed I've never seen in my life, the man backhands Rachel and sends her sliding across the floor. I stifle the urge to tackle him. "The others are on their way…I'll deal with you afterwards," he says to Rachel.

The man turns his attention back toward me. "I am John, the founder of the Dark Crater colony. Tell me what you know."

A thousand lies enter my mind and I quickly focus on what I believe is the best scenario. I put on a show that any actor would be proud of; quivering hands, shaky voice, shaking knees. I'm like a terrified bunny before a ravenous wolf. "I…I thought something strange was going on… I asked her—I begged her to tell me."

"And?"

"And she…she said you were hunters…that you would hunt me down with guns and kill me… I cried until she couldn't stand it anymore. She was going to get me out of here."

John chuckled and said, "Was she now?" He turns his attention back to Rachel. "And what were you planning to do after that?"

Rachel doesn't answer, but I see my chance. I don't know exactly how strong I am now, but I think of trying to smash his spine. It may not kill him, but it might buy us some time. I clench my fist and prepare to thrust.

With a whoosh the doors open and I hold my punch as twenty

men enter the room. They stand at the outer fringes and two walk forward—the captain and the first mate. John looks me in the eyes and holds my gaze. "Rachel told you only a half-truth," he says, "We are going to hunt you, but not with guns."

I keep the charade going. "Then…with what?"

"John stands aside allowing the captain and first mate to step closer. "With these," the captain says, pointing at his teeth, which have grown long and sharp. "Only it won't be me, though I wish it was."

"You'll be my first," the first mate says.

John motions with his head toward the few men standing around Rachel. "Bring her."

Rachel is dragged across the floor and placed next to me. John looks down at her. "Nothing smart to say?"

"You're drunk with power," she says. Something in the statement catches my attention, and I look at the man in a new light. He stands above Rachel, fearless because he imposes fear through violence. I see my father, standing over me with a pipe, striking me down again and again. A drunk bastard. I should have killed him.

"Now that wasn't very smart, was it?" John backhands Rachel again and she slides a few feet away, her skin squeaks against the smooth floor. Only this time, instead of looking down to the ground, she looks John in the eyes.

"You're all cowards!" she says, glaring at the men standing at the fringes of the room. "Every one of you! Do you really think the outside world is going to not notice you forever? Do you really think your crimes against humanity are going to go unpunished forever?

Sooner or later someone's going to come looking for one of your victims, and our colony—a colony of cowards—is going to be found out. Any one of you could change that!"

"No one here is strong enough," John says. "I am the only true-born and there are no first-made among us."

"How convenient for you," Rachel says. "You make the rules. Anyone who can kill you becomes the new leader of DCC, only you don't allow any true-born or..." she glances at me and continues, "first-made to join us."

John nods, "Wisdom of the ages, Rachel. I think I've heard enough." John signals the others. "Prepare them for the hunt."

I know what Rachel wants...for me to kill John, but I don't know how. Anything I do might injure him and not finish the job.

As the men reach for Rachel, she begins to scream. "Please! Someone kill him! Rip out his heart and save the future of the DCC." She puts up a massive struggle taking all attention away from me. John turns his back to me.

Great, now she can read my mind. But I know what I need to do. I know what she wants me to do, but it doesn't seem...human.

I quickly remember that I no longer am human. I embrace my new self and my new abilities. I stand with a speed that no one, including myself, is expecting, and lunge toward John's back.

John's chest explodes out as my fist punches through. There's no scream, no howl of pain, only the gurgle of dripping blood, oozing over my fist, which protrudes through John's ribcage. A few of the men step forward, but stop as I draw my hand back out of John's body.

John's body collapses to its knees and then slumps over forward, leaving me standing above him, still clutching his heart. I feel my own heart beating quicker. My muscles are on fire. I tense as I anticipate an attack. But nothing comes. The men just stand there, silently waiting. Rachel catches my eye and nods.

I drop John's heart onto the floor and say, "Let her go."

The men instantly step away from Rachel. I glare at the captain and first mate and they scurry away like wounded animals, hiding behind the other men. Rachel stands by my side. She takes my hand and squeezes it tightly, filling me with confidence.

"You know the rules," I say, "I'm the boss…and I'm going to make a few changes."

Rachel looks up at me and smiles her smile. It's the last thing I see before my chest explodes. I look down and see my heart, what's left of it, clutched in Rachel's feminine hand.

Damn. Damn. Damn.

I look back to her face, which looks torn. A fire fills her eyes, but her lips are turned sadly down. I swear I see her mouth the word, "sorry," but then I…I think…I…*

AFTERWORD

Despite DARK SEED OF THE MOON being one of the longer stories in this collection, when I first re-read it I had very little memory of why I wrote it. I'm not a huge fan of vampires—I do watch most vampire movies, but have only read three vampire novels, two by David McAfee and one by Jon Merz, and those were after the writing of this story. DARK SEED was also written long before the current vampire craze, so there was no strategic reason to write a vampire story.

But there was a hint of a memory that revealed it wasn't vampires that inspired the story. Rather, it was an article about the moon. NASA believes that craters created by comet impacts on the poles of the moon have remained in a state of permanent shadow—total darkness—and that intergalactic ice may still be there, hiding beneath a coating of moon dust. The idea of eternal night turned my mind to vampires. Because, really, what could be better for sun-shy living dead? Of course, then there is the challenge of feeding on human blood, the answer to which became the plot of this story.

FROM ABOVE

When my arm came off, I knew something wasn't right. It wasn't the pain, because there wasn't any, it was the way it detached from my body—as though a small portion of the world was suddenly freed from the pull of Earth's gravity. It rose up, cut clean, still clinging to my C130 Magnum, and disintegrated, piece by piece until nothing was left. But not just my arm; a perfect circle of the warehouse was carved out as if by a giant, invisible cookie cutter. Everything within the warehouse and the ground beneath that was inside the affected radius simply floated free and then disappeared— atomized. There was no explosion, no twisting of metal or bursting of pipes, it happened as silent as a mouse fart and was over in seconds.

As far as I could tell, I was standing at the edge of ground zero. Another foot forward and I would have joined the three perps I had cornered in the warehouse. Poor bastards were either in deeper than The Authority thought, or they did something to really piss off God.

I looked up and saw the sky; at least it looked clear during the day. A hole, fifty feet wide had been carved into the roof of the warehouse—one of several warehouses I had been checking for Dretch production. Being a narc wasn't my idea of important police work, but some of the hot shots up-town didn't like my style. Of course, that would all change now.

Peering down into the hole, created by whatever invisible force was at work, I came to the realization that this was going to be a big case, maybe the biggest ever. And with me as the only survivor, I'd be back in business.

A tingling in my arm tore my attention away from the gaping hole and thoughts of the future. A stump wiggled below my shoulder. I swore I could still feel my arm moving, but the smell of burnt flesh confirmed my suspicions. Whatever had taken my arm had also cauterized the stump, and it happened so fast that my nervous system didn't even register the catastrophic wound. What was worse, my leathers were ruined.

I decided that I'd find out who took my arm and make sure they paid for what they did. At the very least, they could buy me a new Tac-suit.

That was a year ago. Shit.

Sure, I'm up-town. I've got a new synthetic limb that puts my old arm to shame. But I had to buy my own damn new Tac-suit, and I'm no closer to finding out who put a mile-deep hole in the Earth. The tech-boys tell me it came from an object in orbit, which makes finding the source near impossible. Back in the twentieth century, the human race started putting things in space. Three thousand years later and we haven't stopped. At night it's impossible to tell what's a star and what's some yuppie's space-winni.

A layer of crap, a half mile thick, surrounds the Earth on all sides and bulges at the middle, like the rings of Saturn. And with almost as many people living up there as there are down here, finding out who or what owes me for this Tac-suit is near impossible. The fact that only three wanted felons and my arm were taken makes this case a low priority. Until someone decides to take another potshot at the Earth again, I'm grounded. Not that I'm complaining. My new partner is a fox.

"You on Dretch or something, Priest? Watch the freakin lanes."

Rehna has a way with words that I always enjoy.

I twist the wheel and dodge some old lady driving way too slow for air-trans. She should have stayed on the ground with the rest of the simps. Damn people, afraid of technology. When the human race took to the skies en masse it gave us room to breathe and new freedoms that led to a technological renaissance that lasted for thousands of years. Cities grew up, thousands of feet tall. Vehicles took to the air, traveling faster and safer. Life sped up. Got better.

But not everyone took to the air. Some, afraid of change, stayed on the ground—living slow, unproductive lives; hugging trees, driving cars with wheels and sniffing the damn daisies. Aren't many simps left now-a-days. Good thing too.

"Daydreaming again?" Rehna asks me with a smirk.

"Not about you, so don't get your hopes up." She's gonna love that.

"Do you want me to land and beat you like a school girl?" Her face is turning red. She's either embarrassed or about to shoot me. I decide to find out.

"Keep talking. I think I'm fallin in love."

"That's it." She shoves me to the side and I see her take the wheel, but it doesn't quite register in time to stop what happens next. We're hurtling straight for the ground. My instincts tell me to take the wheel back, to scream, but I know Rehna. She's not suicidal.

Our air-trans mobile unit comes to a stop five feet above the ground, face down. If it were a civilian unit we'd be a smudge on the pavement, but these sleek new mobile units can stop on a dime and cruise at nearly the speed of sound. It's sleek and smooth, the way I like my women, but I can't say I like the light blue color. Kind of *Nancy* if you ask me.

The hatch opens and I fall five feet onto the pavement. She knew I wouldn't be wearing my belt. I hear Rehna's boots hit the pavement behind me. A second later I hear the hum of her C130 warming up. We have a winner. She's gonna shoot me. Now I know I'm falling in love.

"On your feet," Rehna tells me.

I stand and turn to face her; damn she looks hot in a Tac-suit. I gotta remember to thank the man who designed them. They're projectile proof, which is nice, as most perps can't afford C130s. In a pinch can even protect the wearer from the depths of the ocean or the vacuum of space. Not that I've had occasion to test either claim. The point is, in *most* cases, they're nearly indestructible. But the hot laser Rehna's packing will cut through me like a slab of lard. I admire the curves of her body, which are accentuated by the tightness of the black Tac-suit. Her belt hangs loose on her hip...My eyes linger.

"Ugh. That's it," Rehna says. She's losing patience with me. Her C130 falls to the ground. Her belt falls next. This is getting interesting.

Rehna swings high and then low, missing both times. She's fast, I'll give her that. But I've got ten years experience on her, and I can scan her like an unsecured porn server.

"This is stupid," I say, but I don't think it goes through.

I duck two more swings and a third catches my arm. Too bad for her, she picked the wrong arm. *Cling!* My synthetic arm is hard as steel, and she hit it with enough force to knock out a Rhino. Her thick glove keeps her fingers from shattering, and she lets out little more than a stifled grunt. She's tougher than I thought. Her fist comes at me from the other side. I feel a breeze on my chin as her knuckles skim past my face. Too close.

I step back and prepare to end a fight that should have never begun. I told The Authority adding women to up-town was a bad idea. Of course, they didn't listen and now I have to teach Rehna a lesson. One punch to the side should do. Don't want to ruin her pretty face.

As I clench the fist in my human arm, a slight aberration in my vision catches my attention. My memory surges back to the warehouse. I saw the same distortion right before I lost my arm. My eyes track up. A wavering visual phenomenon, like heat rising from hot pavement, cuts straight through the center of a ten thousand foot behemoth, constructed a thousand years ago.

Whack! My check burns with pain after Rehna's punch connects. But my eyes don't leave the sky. Rehna must have noticed, because I don't feel a second punch—good thing too, the first almost broke my jaw. What a woman.

Then it happens. Just like before. Gravity ceases to exist. Half of the behemoth and what looks like miles of other buildings come loose and float toward the sky, turning to dust as they move. Then it's over.

Down the street, I see a hole like the Grand Canyon, but I can't see the other side. It's beyond the horizon. Then I hear the screams; folks panicking, shrieking in fear. We kick into gear and head for the mobile unit. Rehna's in and buckled up in seconds, but two nearby noises catch my attention. Both are whiny—one from above, one from below. I turn to the second and see a little girl, the daughter of some simp probably, but still just a kid.

"Priest, move it! The whole thing's comin down!" Rehna sounds panicked. That's not good.

I look up and see what remains of the behemoth begin to crumble. I run for the girl, arms stretched out. The mobile unit's engines are loud behind me. Rehna's on the ball.

The girl must sense my urgency because she's running for me

now. I scoop her up like a football and look over my shoulder. Rehna's coming on fast. Thank God she left the hatch open. This is going to be close.

I toss the girl back, and she lands hard in my seat. Probably hurt like hell, but at least she'll live. Can't say the same for me though. Let's hope Rehna's reading my mind and doesn't want to kill me.

The mobile unit is on my heels when I jump into the air. I feel the closed hatch sliding beneath me, then the hard metal of the rear casing. I dig my mechanical fingers into the metallic roof and feel a tug as Rehna hits the accelerator, making a beeline for the edge of the city.

Like a falling redwood, the solid building begins to topple above my head, its shadow looming and blocking out the sun. My face begins to sting as dust moving past at one hundred fifty miles-per-hour scours my skin. Rehna must be able to see what I'm seeing. We have ten thousand feet of twisting metal and cement to outrun. As we hit the two hundred mile-an-hour mark, I think about how much of a bitch paper work for today is going to be back at up-town. Then I remember there might not be an up-town left.

We hit four hundred miles an hour, and I'm not thinking anything. My face is burning like its being held against an open flame, and the skin stitched to my synth-arm feels like it's going to tear off. The wind is so loud in my ears I don't hear the explosion as the building hits the ground behind us, leveling miles of city blocks and destroying several other buildings.

The mobile unit slows to a stop somewhere outside of the city. I don't know where, wasn't really paying attention. My forward momentum carries me over the roof and I slide across the hatch, landing on the pavement.

I look up and see Rehna leaning down above me. "You still alive, Priest?"

"Been worse. Help me up."

I stand to my feet and see my reflection in the mobile unit's slick paint job. "Damn."

"What is it?" Rehna asks me.

I look at my Tac-suit, torn and shredded on my body, hanging like a limp corpse. "Now they owe me two Tac-suits."

Rehna smiles.

With most of up-town reduced to atoms there isn't anyone left to report to. Hell, I might be the highest ranking cop in town. All city-bound lines of communication are inoperable, so I turn to the next best source of information. The dashboard sat-link blinks on and is instantly filled with the image of a screaming woman. She appears to be reporting on the wave of destruction that just ravaged my city, but she's incoherent. Useless.

"Channels one through fifty, news filter priority one." The sat-link responds to my voice like an obedient dog, filling the screen with twenty three thumbnail feeds. I scan the images and listen to the mix of voices.

"English only." One by one, images disappear. Only five remain when it's done. Three screens show women reporters crying their guts out. Another displays a man wailing like a stuck pig—embarrassing.

The fifth shows an aerial shot of the carnage, something had carved a clean, perfectly round hole in the center of the city, miles wide and countless fathoms deep. Millions of lives have been lost.

Rehna gasps. "My God."

Women...

The kid is sitting in Rehna's lap, staring intently at the screen, eyes wide. Kid's taking it all in stride. Probably not old enough to be an emotional wreck yet.

"Track five, audio only. Enlarge." The image of the destruction fills the screen.

The voice of a reporter speaks calmly over the feed. "Once again, as it did a year ago, a sinister force from orbit has struck the Earth. The source of the devastation is still unknown and with The Authority headquarters destroyed, chances are, we will never know where and when this evil force might strike again. Scientists studying the clean-cut hole of last year's attack could not identify what kind of weapon was used, only that it is far more advanced than anything in the World District's arsenal. Could technology finally be turning on—"

Before I have time to react, the kid reaches out and messes with the sat-link controls. We lose the feed.

"What the hell, kid? Don't touch this shit," I say, while attempting to readjust the controls.

"Move your damn hand," the kid barks at me.

I stop and give her the coldest stare I can muster—sends most mutts running scared. But the kid just gives it back to me.

"What's your name, kid?"

"Well, it ain't kid."

I wait.

"Gawyn."

"Well, Gawyn. I ain't letting no simp mess with my mobile unit."

"Good. Cause I ain't no simp, old man."

Old man? Kid's looking to get a close up look at my knuckles talking like that. I clench my left fist. Then I feel a squeeze on my shoulder. Rehna's glaring at me. "Let her play with the freakin sat-link, Priest."

I smile. "There you go talking dirty to me again."

Gawyn goes to work. Her fingers are a blur on the screen, working the controls masterfully, faster than I could even with the synth-arm. My eyes widen with every half second, cause that's all it takes for her to access The Authority's satellite mainframe. She's no simp. She's a damn cyber-genius.

"What are you doin, kid?"

"The anti-matter pulse came from orbit."

"Anti-matter pulse?" Rehna's as confused as I am.

"That's just what I call it. I detected its energy field twenty minutes before the pulse. That's how I got out of the target area in time, but just barely."

"You can detect it?" I ask, knowing it's a dumb question.

"Duh. Any kid with an old 40-Gig system and a sat-link could detect it. But you have to look for it. Auto detection won't pick it up as more than a temporary heat-spike."

"And you were looking for it?"

"Since last year." The kid's fingers continue across the controls. She breaches several protected servers and accesses classified surveillance systems. "It's the most kick-ass weapon since the beginning of time."

The kid looks me in the eyes. "You're must be lucky or something. Missed you twice now."

Rehna and I look at each other. "You know who I am?"

"Who doesn't. Your wrinkly face was pasted to every sat-link transmission for a month... Of course, not everyone has been tracking you for the last year. You know, for all your research, you didn't find much."

I look the kid in the eyes and try not to blink. "You've been spying on me for a year?"

"It's not like it's hard, you know." The kid smiles. I have one of the most secure systems in the city. She probably sees it as a playground. Damn kids today. "You've been trying to find out what happened that day...what took your arm, and your Tac-suit. You're obsessed with Tac-suits."

I'm losing patience. "Get to the point."

"When I detected the heat spike, I came to find you. The anti-matter pulse cut the engines off my hyper-scooter. Almost got me too, and I crashed just outside the target area. That's when I found you. I knew that you, more than anyone else, would take action once I told you what I know."

I raise an eyebrow. It's all I'm willing to give.

Gawyn taps one last button on the sat-link. A diagram of Earth orbit and every piece of space junk currently above the city blinks onto the screen. One of the objects is highlighted with a red circle.

"And this is?"

"How'd you ever become a cop?"

Kid's a wise ass. I like her.

Gawyn rolls her neck and speaks quickly. "I figured that if the antimatter pulse fired on this city again that it was probably in a geosynchronous orbit above us."

"Okay..."

"This cuts out bazillions of other possible suspect satellites."

Rehna leans forward. "Meaning we're left with the millions of orbiting objects currently over the city.

"Right, but not everything up there is geosynchronous and the fact that nothing in orbit was destroyed means that what we're looking for is on the bottom layer of a half mile of junk."

Damn kid is smart. Not even the tech-boys could have figured this out. Good thing too, now that they're all dead.

"Now we're left with only a few thousand targets."

"And you've narrowed it down to one?" Rehna asks.

Gawyn nods.

"How?"

"It's hot," I say, finally catching up with the kid.

"Right, but not for long. It's already cooling off."

I activate the hatch and it seals down over us. "What are you doing?" Rehna asks.

"Buckle up," I tell them.

Gawyn looks nervous. "I don't have a seatbelt!"

I smile. "Better double up then."

Rehna and Gawyn wrap a belt around the two of them, and I gun the throttle to the max, pulling more G's than a Disney Universe shuttle pod. I aim for the sky, swerving in and out of airborne traffic—most of it fleeing the city. Three minutes later, we clear ten thousand feet and leave most of the traffic behind.

"Priest, what are you planning to do?" Rehna asks. I can tell she's afraid of the answer. I try to go easy on her.

"Even been in space?" I ask.

Rehna and Gawyn stare at me blankly. The kid explodes, "Bring me back! Bring me back down!"

"I can't," I say as calmly as possible.

"Why not?" Gawyn shouts.

"Cause, kid, I might need you."

Gawyn stares at me. I can feel her trying to gauge my seriousness. Her eyes narrow. "You're right, old man. You do need me."

"I hate to break it to you, Priest, but mobile units aren't rated for space travel." Rehna is trying to remain calm. I'm pretty sure that if the kid weren't on her lap, she might fight me for the controls.

"Actually, that's not entirely true. Up-town might not have let me change the color, but they did let me make a few modifications." I can't help but smile.

"Priest...What modifications?"

I respond by opening a panel next to my right knee. After flipping a switch, the mobile unit beings to shake as loud whirs and clacks emanate from the back. Sounds like we're falling to pieces, but I know better. Rehna screams as we lose power and our ascent slows.

Just as our forward momentum ceases and gravity reclaims its pull on our mobile unit at twenty-five thousand feet, the secondary propulsion unit kicks in, slowly at first, but building in power with each passing nanosecond. Suddenly with a burst of speed, we're flattened against our seats, skin stretching back as we enter Earth's crowded orbit.

For the first time since I've joined the force, I'm wearing my seatbelt. Hard to drive in zero grav when you keep floating off the seat. The kid is having too much fun, working the sat-link upside down, drifting in the cabin. Rehna just looks mortified...or is it pissed? Kind of hard to tell with Gawyn spinning around between us.

"Which way, kid?"

"Gawyn. My name is Gawyn, old man."

"Fine...Gawyn. Which way?"

"Well, Priest, straight-a-freakin-head."

Through the windshield is a mass of floating objects. Some are satellites, serving some purpose to someone. Some are space-decks, orbiting apartment units for people afraid of gravity. The rest is crap—trash tossed into space by folks in the late twenty-first century when they ran out of room for their trash. They figured it would all just float aimlessly through space for all eternity. Dumb bastards didn't count on picking it all back up a year later when they caught up with their own shit. The thought that this is only a year's worth of trash makes me sick.

"Heat signature is faint, but we're within fifty meters," Gawyn says.

All eyes scan the debris field. Some of the trash separates and we enter a clearing, twenty meters wide, twenty tall. Strange.

I cut the gas and we drift forward, toward the center of the clearing, where a satellite floats alone. It's big, the size of an air-bus. At its base, pointed toward the Earth is what appears to be a satellite dish attached to three metallic coils extending out like a solidified DNA sequence.

Fwang! A series of laser blasts ricochet off the mobile unit's hull. The kid jumps back, away from the windshield, but there's nothing to get cranky about. "Ratchet down, Gawyn. Lasers barely left a scratch."

Rehna looks at me, more relaxed now that we're seeing action. "Maybe they'll let you change the paint color now?"

The smile on my face must tell all, because Rehna looks away quickly. Never in my life has a woman remembered something I've said, unless it was an insult. Of course, now might not be the best time to think about it.

Fwang! Fwang! Lasers barrage the outside of the mobile unit doing nothing more than providing a cheesy lightshow. "Must be low yield," I say.

"Probably to deflect space junk," Rehna adds.

I steer us toward the satellite and pull up close next to what looks like a maintenance hatch. Then it occurs to me, this might not just be a satellite...maybe it's a space station. Someone might be alive inside this thing.

As we come within inches of the orbiting beast's hull, the laser fire dies off. Gives me a chance to inspect the outer surface for clues as to who owes me money. "Shit," I say, now knowing I'll never get reimbursed for my Tac-suits.

"What is it?" Rehna asks.

"Mooners," Gawyn spits out. "Dirty Mooners."

Fifteen hundred years ago a moon colony was established and its population grew. Low grav made them multiply like rabbits on Dretch. But their advance in everything techie grew just as fast and they quickly adapted to supporting a massive population. It was one of the most modern facilities ever built and larger than any Earth city at the time. Damn toilets probably wiped their asses for them.

Millions were thriving when Albin was born. The bastard rose to power two hundred years after the colony was formed. He was some kind of religious zealot and fancied himself as God's divine prophet. And the Mooners, ungrateful little whelps, whining about being controlled by us Earthers, staged a brutal and savage revolt. Under Albin's direction, a series of hit-and-run attacks on Earth cities were carried out. The cowards couldn't stand toe to toe with us, so they took aim at normal people, the simps, the young, the yuppies, people who never see the inside of a mobile unit. Killed thousands. They forced Earth to retaliate. Rather than wipe the Mooners clean from the moon with nukes, like I would have done, the government at the time opted to carry out a strategic strike aimed at Albin himself.

A single Earth agent managed to infiltrate Albin's organization and rose to power from within, as a trusted General. Too bad for Albin; he lost his head while taking a crap. A single, high-caliber bullet splattered his brains against the bathroom wall. Got what he deserved too. But he died a martyr. The Mooners continued to piss and moan and soon gained their independence. Not much has been heard from them since. The colony hasn't grown in size. No new construction has been reported...but from the insignia on the outside of this satellite, I now know that they've kept busy over the years.

I attach the docking seal to the side of the satellite—another modification. The sat-link gives the OK and I unbuckle myself and float through the tight opening into the mobile unit's backside. With my new C130 tight in my hand I head for the hatch.

"Wait for me." Gawyn says.

I don't even look back. "Sit your ass back down. No one moves until I say so." I can hear her fold her arms. Must not be used to being told what to do. What I've seen her do with a computer this far leads me to believe she hasn't had much parental supervision. Not that parents are any good for anything other than feeding you.

I open the docking hatch, and a burst of stale air surges into the mobile unit. "Ugh, smells like old farts."

Gawyn's right. Something either died in here or they've got a miniature cow farm tucked inside. At least the air is breathable. "Stay here," I say, as I float forward, into the belly of a beast capable of wiping out entire cities.

Floating inside an orbiting super-weapon isn't something I tend to do often. And the smell has got me spooked—so I lead with my

C130 aimed high. It's cramped inside, like a soda can just big enough for a human. I float through the entrance tube into what must be a cockpit and—holy shit!

I fire my weapon three times with deadly accuracy; two to the chest, one to the head. Too bad the bastard is already dead; shots that precise and that quick would'a gave me braggin rights. But this guy is a rotting heap. His skin is tight and dry, wrapped around his skull like a facelift for the dead. He's probably been here for years, maybe hundreds, with nothing to break down his flesh. Nothing but a human-sized stick of jerky now.

For a dead guy, he packs a lot of attitude. His dried lips are frozen in a sinister grin and his two middle fingers are extended toward the entrance hatch. This guy died knowing he would eventually be found. Definitely Mooners. No one else is this fanatic, to deliver a message hundreds of years after his death. A thought occurs to me; if this guy is dead, who is picking targets and firing this hunk of junk?

"Out of the way, asshole." I take the dead guy by his gray flight suit and toss him to the back of the inner cabin. I hear him hit the wall with a crack. Kind of gives me the creeps, defiling the dead like that, but I'm sure he deserves it.

My body fits in the single cockpit chair nicely. This boat was designed for a single occupant. After scanning the array of controls spread out across three separate panels, I decide I'm screwed. Everything is labeled in some language I've never seen before. So I decide to take a chance and start pushing buttons. The first three do nothing, but the forth opens a front panel, revealing a large windshield and a stunning view of the Earth below. Few people ever get to see the Earth like this, with all the garbage floating in orbit, real estate on the lower levels is near impossible to find. Of course, this view has a flaw. Even from this far away, the clean-cut hole in the Earth, through the heart of my city, can be seen clearly. Gonna make the bastards pay for that.

I reach for another button. "Don't touch that, you idiot!"

I can't remember ever jumping in fright, not even once in my life, but in zero grav I launch out of the seat and hit my head on the ceiling. Embarrassment keeps me from getting angry, as I float above the control panels, looking down at Gawyn. Kid takes my seat at the controls. Probably a good thing too; I might have ended up putting another hole in the Earth.

Rehna floats in through the entrance tunnel. "Sorry, Priest. I tried to stop her."

Gawyn looks up at me. "Can you read Mooner?"

"No."

"Really? No kidding." Gawyn brims with sarcasm. "Cause I could'a sworn you wanted to kill us all."

I don't argue.

Gawyn starts with the magic fingers again. Screens blink to life. The power comes online in full. The air is purified, thank God. I push down from the ceiling to get a closer look at the display screens. Images flash past quickly as Gawyn tears through the complex computer system. Then she stops and looks up at me, floating above her.

"I'm in," she says.

"In where?"

"Mooner city. Their database."

"Kid, you want a job with The Authority, you got it." She smiles, and for the first time I notice she's cute. Not that I go around calling kids cute that often, most of them are about as pleasant looking as an overused snot rag. But Gawyn, she manages to serve a purpose, and she ain't bad to look at, at the same time.

I get lost in my thoughts and fail to notice the changes on the screen. "Priest, are you seeing this?" Rehna asks me.

The screen displays text and images: war machines, tactical gear, a diagram of the Earth with hundreds of orbiting satellites lit up in green. "What the hell?"

Gawyn reads my mind and digs deeper on the satellites. She brings up detailed schematics and tactical information. "Move over," Rehna says, and I push to the side. Rehna can read faster than lightning. One of her eyes was shot out two years back, before I knew her, and she got some new-fangled eye. Lets her scan pages of information like a robot taking snapshots. Rehna scrolls through the information and even the kid can't keep up.

"Holy..." I've never seen Rehna look so stunned. She looks me in the eyes, but the connection I've felt between us is buried deep beneath a sense of dread. "We've got an hour before three hundred of these satellites open fire on the rest of Earth's major cities. Priest, they've been planning this for the last twenty five hundred years."

I roll with the biggest mental punch I've ever received. "The last legacy of Albin. And then what?"

"Invasion."

"So they turn the Earth to Swiss cheese and then invade," I say. "Doesn't sound like the Earth will be worth keeping around."

"It won't be," says Rehna as plain as day.

My eyes widen with the realization that the Mooners don't mean to take over Earth, they mean to destroy it...or at least everyone living on it.

I blink and the kid's back to work, flying her fingers across the consoles, working the keys. "What are you doing?" I ask.

"I ain't letting no Mooners take out my planet," Gawyn replies. "I got friends down there you know."

A loud *hummm* emanates from the rear of the satellite and the walls begin moving around my floating body. She's turning the satellite, aiming at a different target...aiming at the moon. I can't help but smile. This kid's a fighter, but I can't let her be a killer.

"Out of the seat, Gawyn, I'll take it from here."

"But..."

"Now."

Gawyn huffs and floats out of the seat. I resume my place behind the controls. "Okay, now tell me what to do."

Gawyn talks as fast as she types. I do my best to keep up. Within minutes we have the weapon powered up and aimed straight at Mooner central, which Rehna thinks contains the majority of their control centers, population and army, awaiting orders to begin the invasion of Earth. If we're lucky, we can take them all out in one shot.

"Increase the target radius," Gawyn instructs me. "We can take them out in one shot." There she goes, reading my mind again.

As I increase the target radius, a blue bar races across the screen, turning green, yellow, orange and then red. Rehna looks over my shoulder. "Taking a shot that big is going to overload the system. I'd rather not die up here if it's all the same to you."

"If we leave even one control system intact they could still plug the Earth full of holes. I'm not gonna let that happen, even if it kills us all." Rehna doesn't argue, neither does Gawyn. Figures, I'm minutes away from dying and I've finally found a family I could get used to. Oh well.

A vibration tickles my ass beneath the seat as the weapon reaches full charge. I can feel the raw power being built up. Before I can finish my thoughts on how the Mooners were able to leap ahead of us technologically, I see movement in the debris field between us and the moon. Four men in space suits with rocket packs come at us like laser rounds. "We got company," I say plainly.

"Who are they?" Gawyn asks.

"Doesn't matter." I look at their weapons. They look powerful enough to destroy the satellite before we can get a shot off. "Can we set this thing on a timer?"

"I don't know!" Gawyn's starting to panic.

I take her by the shoulders. "You stay here. Set a timer on this thing." I look at Rehna. "Stay with her."

Rehna takes my shoulder as I head for the exit. "Be careful," she says.

What's this mushy stuff? We're trying to save the world from Mooner terrorists and my partner is about to cry over my freakin life, which I have yet to lose and don't intend to lose. Ahh, screw it.

I'm growing tired of being the rude, manly hero anyway. I take Rehna by the waist and pull her toward me, an easy feat in zero grav, and plant a wet one on her lips. I feel my normal stew of negative feelings cool to a light simmer before I pull away. Rehna floats away from me, looking stunned...and stunning. Now I know I love her.

Before Rehna can say something to change my mind, I launch through the docking seal and back into the mobile unit. I fire up the engines and prep the weapons systems. No way I'm gonna let these punks kill my girls.

The assailants pause at the sight of me bearing down on them in a fully armed mobile unit. I don't give them time to figure out what to do. I take aim at the two closest to one another and open up with a lase-sweep. The solid beam of red hot energy slices through space, cutting the two men in half like meat on the butcher's block. The other two rocket away, weaving in and out of the debris field.

They think they're getting away. They're wrong. Obviously, these jokers have never seen what a mobile unit is capable of, or they wouldn't be fleeing in a fairly straight line. Probably think all the junk between me and them will slow me down. Heh, this is going to be fun.

I switch on the mobile unit's auto-defense system and step on the gas. My cannons open up on all sides and unleash Hades. Every hunk of crap within twenty feet is turned into space dust. Anything missed by the cannons, I just plow through. Good thing there's no sound in space or these jokers would hear me coming, like an angry avalanche...with guns. Too much fun.

I lock on to one with an intelrocket. This is gonna scare the crap out of that last guy. The rocket flings through space, dodging debris with incredible agility. Aside from teleporting, there's no way to escape an intelrocket once it's locked on. Two seconds later, the third man explodes in a silent splash of guts, leaving just one more.

He must have seen bits of his friend fly past, because his movements become erratic. Hasn't he learned that shaking me is impossible? The man takes a ninety degree turn and I follow with ease, clearing a wide path for myself the whole way. I lose sight of the man and suddenly burst free of the debris and into a clearing.

Shit! Shit, shit, shit. I should have seen this coming. At the center of the clearing, are what appear to be three Mooner-versions of my mobile unit. They open fire with everything they've got.

I turn hard right and take two hits to my left side. Shakes me up, but I'm otherwise unscathed. After turning off the defense systems, I launch into the debris field, weaving in and out of old satellites and garbage cans. I know I can lose them and it might buy me some time...but for what?

I turn on the com system and try Rehna. "Rehna, this is Priest. You copy?"

"Roger, Priest. We copy. Where the hell are you?"

"Got some unwelcome guests on my tail. How close are you to pulling the trigger?"

"Ready when you are."

Fwash! A laser skims off the hull. Getting closer.

"I want you to wait until I'm in your sights. Then fire that thing, full power."

I hear the kid grab the line. "You can't! That's crazy!"

"Shut-up, kid." No time to play wet-nurse. "Pull the trigger or I'm gonna die anyway." I hang up, not in the mood for goodbyes.

After entering the path I carved earlier, I floor it, pouring on the speed like a cybernetic cheetah. They're right on my ass. Fast little bastards. I make a beeline for the Mooner-weapon's attack zone and set the controls: straight ahead, full speed. I take my biohazard mask from its compartment and strap it to my head. Might help me survive.

I pick up the com. "Rehna?"

"We're ready, Priest," she replies, voice wavery.

"I need you to go ahead and open the outer airlock doors."

She responds just the way I like it. "Done."

"Be ready to seal the airlock on my signal."

"What signal?"

"You'll know."

Bachoom! A shot hits me directly in the rear. Then another and another. Better make this quick.

"Priest, you got five seconds before we fire."

I pop the hatch and it floats away at five hundred miles per hour. I push off the floor and float out of the cab at the same speed, as I enter the target area. The three Mooner ships continue after the mobile unit, guns blazing. Probably thought I was a piece of shrapnel they blew off. Their mistake, my salvation.

Reaching out with my synth-arm, I wield a grappling hook,

which I launch toward the Mooner satellite. It finds its home, embedded in the metal hull and catches tight. At five hundred miles per hour, even in space the pull is incredible. It takes all of my cybernetic strength to hold on, as I swing wide, out of range. A second later, my vision blurs as the weapon fires and the three Mooner ships cease to exist, along with my mobile unit.

My chest begins to burn. I'm longing to take a breath, but I know if I do, I'll just suck in the cold of space. The face mask over my eyes holds nicely and gives me the ability to aim where I'm going, spinning around the satellite, over and over again like a wild tetherball getting closer and closer to the pole. My speed slowed at first, but has picked back up with every revolution. This is gonna hurt.

On my last revolution, I can tell that my aim was true. Instead of slamming into the outer hull, I'm about to be flung inside the open airlock. I lead with my synth-arm, letting it take the majority of the impact and using it to slow the rest of my body before I slam into the airlock doors.

The impact knocks the wind out of me and I feel desperate to suck in air. But I know if I do, I'm dead. My vision starts going black, and I concentrate on keeping my mouth shut, clenching my jaw. I feel hands grab my shoulders and pull, but it's the last thing I sense.

I wake up ten minutes later to the sound of Gawyn yelling up a blue streak. "What are we gonna do! We're gonna be splattered!"

After opening my eyes, I quickly survey the situation. Through the windshield I see the Earth spinning below and coming up quick. I must have knocked the satellite out of orbit when I hit. Better lay off the cheeseburgers.

My stomach turns as I feel gravity begin to take control. A sudden jerk pulls me off the floor, and I fall down the now vertical satellite. I fall past Gawyn and Rehna, and slam onto the windshield, face down. I open my eyes to a close-up view of the Earth's surface. But now it's approaching more slowly.

I roll over onto my back and face Gawyn and Rehna, their eyes wide. "I think it's safe to say this thing has a parachute."

"And hard freakin glass," Gawyn says with a smile.

I smile back. Kid's making me all warm and freakin fuzzy. Maybe I'll retire.

After twenty minutes of floating through the sky, we land back in the city, on the top of one of the few remaining ten thousand foot buildings. Popping the hatch proves a challenge for my weary and burning muscles, but my synth-arm is still up to the task. We're greeted by the cool night air, kept clean and breathable by air scrubbers running up the sides of every building in town. I suck the air in like a siphon.

The girls climb down the side of the satellite one at a time, both refusing my help. I'm just shocked that I offered to begin with. As I roll my neck back, letting the bones crack back into place, I notice how bright the stars are. Stars... I laugh as I realize that when the weapon was fired it cleared a clean hole over the city. Probably killed a bunch of civies in the process, but you know what they say about breaking a few eggs.

My vision follows the stars to a bright object floating in space that I've only seen in books. The moon. With all the crap orbiting the planet, no one on the surface has seen the moon for a thousand years. Probably just the way they liked it, being able to move in concealment, like sneaking up on a scared kid hiding under the blankets. Too bad for them, this scared kid got hold of a big gun.

A perfectly round hole, the size of Maine, stares back from the Moon's surface—evidence that any threat from the moon has been wiped out. Any Mooner forces remaining are probably scattering in a confused daze, unsure where to run. Rehna and Gawyn stand next to me, staring up in silence.

"Hard to believe we did that." Rehna says.

I look her in the eyes. "Think they'll let me go back up there and turn it into a smiley face?"

She just smiles back and takes my hand. Feels funny, but I let it linger. A pressure on my finger brings my eyes back down, and I see Gawyn holding onto my index finger. My muscles tense and I fight the urge to shrug them both off, but after wiping out an entire civilization, I've destroyed enough lives for one day. I pick the kid up and throw her over my shoulders. With my arm around Rehna, I head for the roof stairwell, thinking about starting a new life. Maybe I'll get a dog too.

Heh, I'm all freakin heart.

AFTERWORD

My editor recently described this story as noir. My immediate internal reaction was, "What?! No! I hate noir!" Having reread the story, I see that he's right. While sci-fi noir is not something I would consciously write, it seems a part of me appreciates the genre. My only memory of actually writing this story is being in between novels, having a few hours to spare and sitting down in front of my laptop.

As an artist, I often sit down with a blank piece of paper and just start drawing. I don't know what I'm going to draw. I just start putting lines on the page and something emerges. It's not some kind of metaphysical experience, I just see something in the shape and expand upon it. I play the same game with my family while waiting for food in the restaurant. Someone scribbles some quick lines, and I turn it into a drawing. The creation of FROM ABOVE was similar. I sat down and started dreaming up good first lines. After a few minutes I typed, "When my arm came off, I knew something wasn't right."

I built the rest of the story around that line, first explaining how it had happened and then asking and answering the follow-up questions that explanation created. The story emerged on its own, and I suspect the noir feeling of it comes from it being written that way. I was asking and answering questions like a detective and that voice crept into my writing.

The end result is an experimental story that turned into my first magazine-published piece and made me a whopping fifty bucks.

BOUGHT AND PAID FOR

One hundred feet below ground, knee deep in unrefined, pure shit, Jonas Flynn laughed. The key in his hand, ancient and rusted, had worked.

He had entered the sewer line two miles down and slogged his way through what looked like a fecal parade, on a river of piss, bile and rancid water. The mask he wore enabled him to breath, but its ill fit allowed the occasional waft of sewer air in. It wasn't the smell that got him. It was the *taste*.

But it'd all been worth it. He was in. Every security system had a weakness, back door or secret entry. The Navy mainframe's Achilles heel happened to be buried fifty feet underground, in a sewer line that ran beneath Navy Intelligence's fallout shelter. A *long forgotten* fallout shelter. If you went back in time far enough, even the best-kept secrets could be retraced forward and discovered in the present.

It was the basic principle of private investigations, at which he excelled. Though what was now considered private investigation had once been known as hacking and typically involved computers, not sewers. But he'd get to that.

Jonas made his living by scouring the virtual sewers online and in people's private systems. No secret was safe. Except, as fate would have it, the one fucking secret that really mattered—the location of Walter Elly.

The metal hatch groaned as Jonas pulled it open. Chips of rust fell from the hinges, landing in the toxic sludge at Jonas's knees. He shined his flashlight inside. The tunnel was long, small and thank God, dry. He climbed into the tunnel, shimmied inside a few feet and kicked off his waders. He would need them for the trip back out.

He crawled through the tunnel, pulling himself forward by his forearms. He tried to look up, but his head smashed into the ceiling. He cursed, slammed his fist down, then continued forward, never knowing how much further he had to go. The schematics had shown the tunnel to be only one hundred feet long before meeting the vertical tube that lead up to the fallout shelter, but his slow pace made it seem much longer.

As he pushed forward, his thoughts turned to Elly. He knew very little about the man: what he looked like (5'8, skinny but strong, and a cocky shit-eating grin), his name, rank and his Navy serial number. He'd ripped the dog tags from Elly's neck when he pulled the man off of Kira, Jonas's dead wife. What had followed was still a blur. He'd taken Elly by surprise, knocked him to the kitchen floor next to Kira's body and stomped on the man's face until he lay motionless.

He didn't stomp hard enough.

Elly survived.

After the police arrived, Elly came to. When they dragged him away, Elly flashed a near-toothless version of his shit-eating grin and whispered, "Check the bedroom."

Seeing his wife dead on the kitchen floor, stabbed nine times with a bowie knife, had been hard enough for Jonas. Finding his children, ages three and five, strangled and discarded in a heap had broken something inside him. He wouldn't just kill Elly, he'd torture him—kill him as painfully and slowly as possible. It became his life's goal. He put all his money and resources into the task, but Elly had disappeared. The police records showed that he was transferred to a Navy prison, but they didn't know which one.

The dog tags were his only clue. Fortunately, thanks to a memory augmentation, Jonas would never forget the information. *Could* never forget it. Elly's name, rank and serial number would be with him forever.

He'd been up the virtual skirt of every Navy system he could find, but there wasn't any mention of Elly, past or present. The man disappeared. Like he never existed.

Just like my family.

Jonas pulled himself forward on his now raw left arm, bringing his right up over and down again, but there was no floor to support him. He lurched forward as his arm fell over the edge of a vertical drop. His flashlight fell away, spinning a beam of light, as it fell into the darkness below. He watched the flashlight fall until it was a speck of light. He never heard it hit the bottom.

He cracked a glow-stick that lit the tunnel in a cool blue. The ladder was right where it was supposed to be. He took hold of the nearest metal rung and pulled himself out of the tunnel. When his feet came clear, his lower half swung down. But he was expecting the drop and landed square on the ladder, which seemed free of rust. He bounced on the ladder. It held tight.

He climbed.

Ten minutes later he reached the top, out of breath and with aching knees. A metal hatch, identical to the one on the sewer line, waited for him. The only difference between the two hatches was that this one was free of rust. Fitting the key into the lock would take no finagling this time. He inserted the key, turned it and opened the door. The air beyond was musty, but breathable. With the glow stick in his mouth, he climbed through the hatch and into a small metal chamber where a second, full-sized metal door waited.

This is where his plan ventured into the unknown. The fallout shelter on the other side was hardwired to the Navy Command above, which would give him access to the computer systems behind the hardware firewall, which he'd been unable to bypass from the outside. That would be easy. But this door required brute force. Jonas preferred finesse, but there was no other way. He pulled two small devices from his cargo pants pocket. On the black market they were known as DIGs (Destruction Is Guaranteed) and they'd cost the better portion of his remaining savings. But he was assured that just one could open any door. To be sure, he'd bought three.

He duct-taped two of the explosives to either side of the door, set the timers for thirty seconds, and returned to the ladder. With fifteen seconds to spare, he closed and relocked the outer hatch, tightened his grip on the ladder and waited.

The explosion dwarfed all of his expectations. The walls above him shot out, as a plume of debris smashed against the far wall and then descended the pit like a pyroclastic cloud. Through the dust, Jonas looked up and saw the thick metal hatch lean out toward him, then fall. It struck his shoulder, breaking his collar bone and then tumbled into the abyss.

Though his entire left side now groaned with pain, Jonas repositioned his mask and breathed freely in the dust. When the dust settled, he made his way back up, struggling to hold onto the rungs with his injured arm. He slid onto his belly, then stood. The metal door was gone, along with the walls, a portion of the ceiling and most of the room beyond.

"Guess I should've used just one," he said.

The space beyond was a storage room. Thick liquids oozed from stacks of old canned goods. Bags of rice hissed at him as their contents slid to the floor. He made his way through the room, kicked down the bent door at the opposite end and entered a hallway. He cracked two more glow sticks and read the labeled doors as he walked past. He stopped at: *Communications*.

He tried the door. Unlocked.

A pair of old computers sat unused since their installation, yet they were miraculously dust free. Jonas wouldn't have been surprised if they still worked, but he wasn't after the computers. He knelt below the table and looked at the wall. The ports were ancient. T-17s. But he'd come prepared. After stretching out his screen and unrolling the keyboard, he took out a key ring that held fifty-odd adapters. He found the right one, plugged in and powered on.

Less than two minutes from the moment his screen collected and joined the microscopic particles in the air and projected the image of a Navy login screen, Jonas had the information he'd been looking for. Elly had been transferred—not to a brig, but to a battleship. The Keeling. He was serving as a...a pilot?

"What the fuck?"

What kind of justice was that?

Not his kind.

Jonas pursued the line of inquiry. He needed to find out everything he could about the Keeling.

"What the fuck!"

He found nothing.

Increasing his search parameters to the Keeling and Walter Elly turned up a single document. A crew manifest. Elly was on it. As were hundreds of other men and women, from Captain Antoine Williams to deck hand Peter Molitor. He began researching each individual crew member. His fingers flew over the keyboard and his eyes scanned the screen. An hour later he'd absorbed the details of each and every crew member, past and present, who had ever served on the Keeling. While researching, he'd been collecting the data, storing it in his perfect memory, but he had yet to process it. When he sat back, rubbed his eyes and thought about what he'd read, he smiled.

This was going to be easy.

Jonas worked the keyboard again, but this time he wasn't simply reading information, he was creating a new file. His file. A military record. Time in the Navy. He knew the positions that needed to be filled—the Keeling seemed to go through crew quickly—and he knew what he could pass for. The galley needed a cook. He'd be the perfect candidate. 41 years old, though his bald top and grey sideburns made him look older. A little thick around the middle, but tough and good in the kitchen. He crafted his tour of duty, record and history to fit the perfect mold. When he was finished, he was a new man—Samuel Draper.

Now all he needed to do was kill someone.

Draper left the shelter, but he didn't take the same path out that Jonas had taken in. Instead he headed up. First through four sub-basements. Then through a storage level. He passed a few workers who gave him odd glances, but he continued undisturbed, while they talked about the small earthquake they'd felt. Upon reaching a service elevator, he took it to the first floor. He exited into the lobby where a receptionist waited.

He walked quickly to the desk, smiled and said, "Hi there..." He read her name tag, "Nancy." I just came up from Sublevel 5 and noticed something odd in the elevator. Can you come tell me what you think it is?"

She eyed him for a moment, but his smile and deep blue eyes won her over. "This better not be a joke."

"No joke, I swear."

He led her to the elevator and pushed the call button. The doors slid open. A small device sat on the floor of the elevator. "There it is," he said.

"Why, I don't know..." Nancy knelt down and picked up the object. "There are numbers on it."

"What numbers?"

She held it up, showing him the red, digital numbers displayed on a small screen.

15

14

13

She looked at the numbers again. Her eyes went wide. "It's a countdown!"

His fist struck the side of her head before she could flee. She went down hard, whimpering in pain.

"I'm sorry," he said. "There was no other way."

As the doors closed, he stepped out of the elevator and dove to the side. The explosion chased him, but didn't penetrate the metal box. The doors and walls all bent outwards, but the force of the explosion remained contained, putting all of its energy into Nancy's body. When the klaxons rang out and the Navy Guard showed up, they pried the doors open. The interior of the elevator had been painted red, blemished by the occasional charred chunk of flesh and bone.

Draper pled guilty on the spot and was thrown in the brig. His ticket to the Keeling had been bought and paid for. Samuel Draper would have his revenge.

AFTERWORD

A few years ago, Scott Sigler, horror writer extraordinaire and friend, came to me with a request. He was putting together a podcast novel (free audiobook) called THE CRYPT. To add to the story, and help build interest, he was asking other authors to write short stories that created the characters for the novel and revealed their motivation for being on the spaceship referred to as The Crypt (because most who served on the ship, died on the ship).

BOUGHT AND PAID FOR is my contribution to this collaborative effort, and Sigler said it was the fan favorite out of the bunch. If you enjoyed this story, and would like to learn more about Jonas's fate, visit:

http://www.scottsigler.com/taxonomy/reverse/71.

You can listen to all of the character intros, including BOUGHT AND PAID FOR, as well as the entire novel, FOR FREE.

Please enjoy a sample from Jeremy Robinson's
THE LAST HUNTER - DESCENT

—SAMPLE—

THE LAST HUNTER by JEREMY ROBINSON
Available on Kindle, Nook, and Smashwords, as well as in trade
paperback format.

DESCRIPTION:

I've been told that the entire continent of Antarctica groaned at the
moment of my birth. The howl tore across glaciers, over mountains
and deep into the ice. Everyone says so. Except for my father; all he
heard was Mother's sobs. Not of pain, but of joy, so he says. Other
than that, the only verifiable fact about the day I was born is that an
iceberg the size of Los Angeles broke free from the ice shelf a few
miles off the coast. Again, some would have me believe the fracture
took place as I entered the world. But all that really matters, accord-
ing to my parents, is that I, Solomon Ull Vincent, the first child
born on Antarctica—the first and only Antarctican—was born on
September 2nd, 1974.

If only someone could have warned me that, upon my return to
the continent of my birth thirteen years later, I would be kidnapped,
subjected to tortures beyond comprehension and forced to fight...and
kill. If only someone had hinted that I'd wind up struggling to

survive in a subterranean world full of ancient warriors, strange creatures and supernatural powers.

Had I been warned I might have lived a normal life. The human race might have remained safe. And the fate of the world might not rest on my shoulders. Had I been warned....

This is my story—the tale of Solomon Ull Vincent—The Last Hunter.

EXCERPT:

Chapter 12

My foot rolls on a bone as I kick away from the bodies. There's so many of them, I can't make out what I'm seeing. It's like someone decided to play a game of pick-up sticks with discarded bones. I fall backwards, landing on a lumpy mass. My hands are out, bracing against injury. Rubbery flesh breaks my fall, its coarse hair tickling between my fingers. I haven't seen the body beneath me, but I know—somehow—that it's dead.

Long dead.

This is little comfort, however. After finding my footing, I stand bolt upright. My chest heaves with each breath. Each draw of air is deep, but the oxygen isn't getting to my head. I try breathing through my nose, and the rotten stench of old meat and something worse twists my stomach with the violence of a tornado. I drop to one knee, fighting a dry heave.

"Slow down," I tell myself. "Breathe."

I breathe through my mouth. I can *taste* the foul air, but I force each breath into my lungs, hold it and then let it out slowly. Just like I learned at soccer practice. I only lasted a few practices before giving up, but at least I came away with something. Calm down. Focus. Breathe.

My body settles. I'm no longer shaking. But when I look up I wonder if I've done something wrong. Stars blink in the darkness, like when you stand up too fast. But they're not floating around. They're just tiny points of light, like actual stars, but I get the feeling they're a lot closer. The brightest of the light points are directly behind me, and to test my theory I reach out for them. My hand strikes a solid wall.

Stone.

The points of light are small glowing stones, crystals maybe. I'd be fascinated if I weren't absolutely terrified.

My hand yanks away from the cool surface as though repulsed by a magnetic force. For the first time since waking, a rational thought enters my mind.

Where am I?

It's a simple question. Finding the answer will give me focus. I turn my mind to the task while my body works the adrenaline out of its system.

The dull yellow stars behind me are large, perhaps the size of quarters. They wrap around in both directions, almost vanishing as they shrink with the distance. But I can see them surrounding me with a flow of tiny lights. There is no door. No escape.

I'm in a pit.

Full of bodies.

Long dead bodies, I remind myself as my breathing quickens. It's like looking at the mummies in The Museum of Fine Arts. *They can't hurt you.*

With my eyes better adjusted to the dim light, I crouch down to look at the bone I stepped on. What I see causes me to hold my breath, but I find myself calming down for two reasons. First, my mind is engaged, and like Spock, my emotions, which can overwhelm me, are being choked out. Second, the bones are not human.

The nearest limb looks like a femur, but it's as thick as a cow's and half the length. I try to picture an animal that would have such thick, short limbs, but nothing comes to mind.

I scan the field of bones. Most are similar in thickness and size, but many I can't identify. Whatever these bones belonged to, I'm fairly certain they're not human. In fact, they don't belong to any creature I've ever seen before.

Remembering the soft flesh that broke my fall, I turn around and look down. If not for the clumps of rough red hair sticking out of the sheet of white skin, I might have mistaken it for a chunk of rug padding. The skin is thick, perhaps a half inch, and hasn't decomposed at all despite the bones beneath it being free of flesh.

A scuff above me turns my head up as dirt and dust fall into my face. Someone is above me.

"Who's there?" My voice echoes.

The only response I get is silence, which makes me angry. I've been beaten and kidnapped after all. "Hey! I know you're there!"

"I wouldn't do that if I were you."

The sinister scrape of the voice makes my stomach muscles tighten. This is the man who took me.

"Why?" I ask through clenched teeth, determined not to show this man fear.

"Because..." I suspect his pause is for dramatic effect. When I feel the sudden urge to pee, I know it's working. "...you're not alone."

I spin around, forgetting all about my bladder. I can't see more than ten feet of body-strewn floor. Beyond that it's just a sea of light flecks. If there is someone down here with me, I'll never see them.

Then I do.

In the same way we detect distant objects moving in space, I see a body shifting to my left, blocking out the small lights.

"Who is it?" I whisper.

"Not a who," answers the voice.

Not a who? *Not a who*!

"What am I supposed to do?" My whisper is urgent, hissing like the man's voice.

"Survive. Escape."

"How?"

"That's up to you." I hear him shuffling away from the edge. His voice fades as he speaks for the last time. "I will not see you again until you do."

A rattle of bones turns my attention back to the sneaking shadow. My eyes widen. It's no longer slinking to the side. It's growing larger, blocking out more and more stars. That's when I realize it's not growing larger, it's getting closer.

In the moment before it strikes, I hear it suck in a high pitched whistle of a breath. I duck down to pick up the thick bone that tripped me up. But it's too late. The thing is upon me.

Chapter 13

I scream.

I'm too terrified to do anything else. My hands are on my head. I'm pitched forward. My eyes are clenched shut. Every muscle in my body has gone tight, as though clutched in rigor.

It knocks me back and I spill into a pile of bones and old skin. But I feel no weight on top of me. No gnashing of teeth on my body. The thing has missed its tackle, striking a glancing blow as it passed, but nothing more. Perhaps because I bent down. Perhaps because it can't see well in the dark. I don't know. I don't care.

I'm alive. For now.

And I don't want to die.

But I'm certain I'm going to and the events of the past few months replay in my mind. I can't stop it. I can't control it. And in a flash, I'm back at the beginning. A moment later, my mind returns to the present. I'm still in the pit. Still waiting for death. But I feel different somehow.

My attention is drawn down. The thick bone is still in my hand. I stand, holding it at the ready like Hercules's club or Thor's hammer. What I wouldn't give for an ounce of their strength right now.

But strength is something I lack. I can already feel my limbs growing weak from fright. If this fight doesn't end quickly I'll probably lie down and accept death like a deer in the jaws of a mountain lion. It always amazes me how quickly prey animals accept their fate once caught. Will I be any different?

The answer surprises me.

A shift of shadow to my left catches my eye. But this time the fear is drowned out by a rage I have felt before, a rage that now has an outlet. I lunge for the shadow, bone-club raised. The thing flinches back, surprised by my attack. My first swing misses, nearly spinning me around. But I follow it up with a backhand swing worthy of John McEnroe. The impact hurts my arm, but it lets me know I've hurt the thing, too.

The thing stumbles back, letting out a high pitched whine as it strikes the wall. I struggle to see it, but it's backlit by the wall. I can, however, see its silhouette more clearly now. Its body is egg-shaped and maybe four feet tall, with short, thick legs. Its arms are almost comical—short stubs sticking out to either side as useless as a T-Rex's tiny appendages. I feel emboldened by the thing's size and awkward build. But I've underestimated its will to live. This thing doesn't want to die as much as I don't.

It lets out a shrill scream and charges again. I start to duck, but this time it doesn't leap. Instead, it lowers its top half—I can't see where the head begins or ends or if it even has a head—and plows into me like a battering ram. It lifts me off the ground and carries me ten feet before slamming me into a stone wall. I hear a crack as my head strikes, but I don't lose consciousness. There's too much adrenaline in my system for that to happen.

But when I open my eyes and look at the thing, I wish I had fallen unconscious. Then I wouldn't have seen it. I wouldn't be awake when it devoured me. But I am awake, staring into a set of jaws that looks like it belongs to a great white shark—rows of serrated triangular teeth set into a jaw that protrudes from the mouth. The entire top half of the creature, just above its pitiful arms, has opened up to take me in. I have no doubt I'll be severed in half. I'll spend my last living moments bleeding out in this thing's gullet.

I can't die like this.

"Get off of me!" I scream. My voice distracts the creature. Its jaws close slightly, revealing a pair of perfectly black eyes, like two eight balls jammed into the top of a killer Humpty Dumpty. Tufts of thick brown hair cover its milky skin.

I've seen this before. The remains of these creatures litter the cave floor. These things aren't killing people here, they're being killed. It wasn't put here to kill me, I was put here to kill *it*.

"Get off me, I said!" I shout, further confusing the beast. I dive to the side, but it clamps down on my shirt—a red, white and blue flannel that looks much more patriotic than any piece of clothing should. I spin around and lose my balance. The shirt rips as I fall away. My hands stretch out to brace my fall and I plunge into a litter of bones—the bones of this thing's kin. But my right hand catches on something sharp. A hot burn strikes my palm, followed by a warm gush of liquid over my wrist.

I'm bleeding.

And the thing can smell it. I hear its quick breaths, sniffing as a dog does. Then I hear the smacking of lips and then it moves again, closing in on me.

Ignoring the pain in my hand, I dig into bones and find the sharp object. Playing my fingers over it gently, I feel a large triangular tooth. Then another. And another. In my mind's eye I can see its shape: a broken jawbone from one of these creatures. I find an end that has no teeth and grip it.

I'm back on my feet for only a moment before the creature charges again. But I'm ready for it. Whatever this thing is, it's deadly, but it's not smart enough to realize I would anticipate the same attack.

I step to the side and swing down. I feel an impact, and then a tug on my weapon as the teeth catch flesh. A sound like tearing paper fills the air and makes me sick to my stomach. I can't see it, but I know I have just sliced open the creature's back.

It whimpers and stops.

I step closer.

It steps away.

Some instinct I never knew I had tells me I've inflicted a mortal wound. The thing is dying. I see its form again as it nears the far wall—egg shaped body, tiny arms, squat legs, large eyes. And I recognize it for what it is. Not the species, the age.

It's a baby.

I've just killed a baby.

As it mewls against the wall, each call weaker then the last, the jaw-weapon falls from my hand.

"No," I whisper, falling to my knees. What kind of a sick world have I been brought to?

I want my mother.

I scream for her. "Mom!" I scream again and again, my voice growing hoarse. My face is wet with tears and snot. My body is wracked by sobs between each shout for my mother. My thoughts turn to my father. How awful he must feel now that I'm gone, knowing I disappeared while angry with him. Not only had he lied to me for thirteen years, but he also believed I was capable of hurting Aimee. He didn't trust me. Never had. But I trusted him now. *Was this what he was protecting me from?* This thought strikes me like a fist and I long for my father's presence. He could protect me. I yell for him next.

But he doesn't come. He can't hear me. He'll never hear me again. How could he?

My voice fades to a whisper. Pain stabs my head with every beat of my heart. The pinpricks of light surrounding me are now blurry halos. In the quiet, I can no longer hear the ragged breathing of the young creature. Certain it's dead, I weep again, mourning not just the death of this deformed thing that tried to eat me, but the death of something much more precious to me: my soul. As my body gives way to exhaustion, I slide down onto the stone floor, surrounded by bones and wonder, *maybe that's the point.*

ABOUT THE AUTHOR

JEREMY ROBINSON is the author of ten thrillers including Pulse and Instinct, the first two books in his exciting Jack Sigler series. His novels have been translated into nine languages. He is also the director of New Hampshire AuthorFest, a non-profit organization promoting literacy in New Hampshire, where he lives in New Hampshire with his wife and three children.

Connect with Robinson online:
www.jeremyrobinsononline.com

CPSIA information can be obtained at www.ICGtesting.com
Printed in the USA
LVOW04s1920250813

349506LV00004B/820/P